Murder, Mayhem And Monet

Karen Hudgins

A Wings ePress, Inc.
Mystery Novel

Wings
Press, Inc.

Wings ePress, Inc.

Edited by: Jeanne Smith
Copy Edited by: Rebecca Smith
Executive Editor: Jeanne Smith
Cover Artist: Trisha FitzGerald-Jung

All rights reserved

Wings ePress Books
www.wingsepress.com

Published In the United States Of America

Wings ePress Inc.
3000 N. Rock Road
Newton, KS 67114

What They Are Saying About

Murder, Mayhem and Monet

A suspenseful mystery set in one of my favorite Colorado mountain towns. I could picture myself walking the tourist beat alongside Diane trying to solve this whodunit. Great characters, fun twists, with a little are history thrown in to make this a winner!
—Karen Bunce Sheff, Reader & (former) Business Educator

Mayhem is the secret to a cleverly plotted maze of characters, misdirection, and ambiguous clues that keep the reader wondering what the next chapter will bring. The solution is tidy and the denouement is the perfect finishing touch!
—Virginia Vendt, Reader & former university librarian

Got sucked into *Murder, Mayhem, and Monet* completely! The story simmers all the way through; plot twists, and possibilities charge the air...and delivers a power punched ending. WELL DONE!
—Ron Martin, Reader, Writer, and Artist

This great weekend read gave me not only new friends to meet in its pages, but also a glimpse into the art of Monet that I hadn't known. The characters layered on more depth, as the story progresses, and drew me into their world. It was just as fun seeing in my mind's eye the richness of the town, and the search for the truth unfold, as it was meeting the people who told the story.
—Debby Steele, Reader

Murder, Mayhem and Monet is a whodunit mystery, and it does not disappoint! I especially liked Diane Phipps, P.I., and rooted for her the entire time as she methodically collected information and zeroed in on suspects. Manitou Springs made for an interesting setting with the wintry weather, trails, and views. I could almost taste Diane's hot chocolate after she came inside from a wintry storm. Karen has created a light, enjoyable mystery with plenty of twists, turns, and unexpected surprises! Enjoy!

—Pegeen B., Reader, Author

Dedication

For Kathleen Coddington, Vicki Ferguson, Rosemary Pennell,
Allison Hawkins,
and Janet Bellanger

Prologue

Nothing could excite Arabella Lauren more than restoring one of Claude Monet's "Waterlilies" to its flawless beauty. With barely taking time for coffee, she'd arrived at her second-floor studio in the Falcon Building in Manitou Springs. She took off her coat and turned on the lights that warmed the exposed brick walls. Stepping over to the window, she opened the blind slats and gazed down at Manitou Avenue.

Her home town was awakening for business, and street parking was already filling up. People, mostly residents, were bundled up as snow had fallen again last night. By summer, she'd not be able to see much of the pavement because of the crowds.

Occasionally, folks slowed or stopped for window shopping. Hank, the fudge maker at the candy store, Sunny, the t-shirt shop owner, and Willa, the local smoky crystal purveyor hustled to work. Strangers or not, other walkers passed each other, giving nods or

1

sharing words. This town was a friendly place, where mostly parking tickets or peace disturbances kept law enforcement busy.

With a slow draw, Arabella pulled the cord to raise the blinds and allowed as much light in as possible. She walked to the next window and did the same and then to the last one for good measure. Except for direct sun, natural light couldn't be more valuable in her work.

Directly across the street from her studio, her friend Pam Piper was entering the front door to her jewelry shop. That meant it was 9:45 a.m., or only fifteen minutes until Arabella's special delivery would arrive. It was also Tuesday, so she and Pam would have lunch together up the street at The Loop.

About to turn away, Arabella stilled. Someone else she knew— *had known so well*—ambled into view. Wearing jeans and a leather jacket with the Italian boots she'd bought him for his birthday, he stopped at the trash bin. Looking up at her windows, he tossed a coffee cup into the bin.

Despite it all, a tug pulled her heart over his good looks. She'd long been an appreciator of beauty in all its forms. Besides, he was the man she'd once pinned her dreams on. In the end, though, she'd left him. His beauty was truly only skin deep. Now there he was, checking out her place. Back home from an extended trip, she figured. Unsmiling, he abruptly turned and walked west.

Arabella stepped left and watered a red geranium on the sill. At 10:00 a.m. sharp, the driver of a nondescript van secretly carrying the priceless cargo pulled into the side alley of the Falcon. She could hear the vehicle backing onto the aging delivery dock.

Arabella left the spacious studio via the back elevator. Soon standing on the cold concrete dock, she waved him into the narrow space. Her heart thumped with excitement. Ready for hours of special painstaking work that lay ahead, she had worn comfortable clothes.

Her thick grey knit sweater covered the top of non-designer jeans, and worn soft boots warmed her feet. A silk scarf with colorful butterflies hung loosely around her neck. Her slim black apron with little pockets touched her knees. She adjusted her tortoise-framed glasses, and the incoming breeze fluttered her chestnut hair over her face.

The driver turned off the engine, returning peace to the neighboring shops, eateries, and galleries. She met the high-security courier at the top of the short flight of steps after he'd hopped from the van with a helper, both dressed in jumpsuits. He presented her with a clipboard with forms to sign and tugged on his cap. A holstered pistol sat at his right hip.

Despite the cold and her excitement, Arabella held her hand surprisingly steady while signing. She had much practice with steadiness of hand, much like a surgeon—which she had once considered as a career. But her passion for saving fine art had won out over the medical arts. Her brother Leo had given his career life to chemistry. When discussions rose during family gatherings, she reminded everyone that chemistry played a crucial role in the restoration of pigments to their original brilliance and colors. She'd just made a career side-step, which kept her happy.

Then came the day Leo got interested in collecting art. Lo and behold, some of it needed cleaning. So, with whom did he contract the work to be done? His sister, Arabella Laurens, Fine Art Restoration. Although they often didn't see eye-to-eye, he was duly impressed with her work. So far, she had no disappointed clients and meant to keep it that way, particularly with the Monet masterpiece arriving at her studio.

When the rarely seen Monet had been "found" after years of storage in a remote French village barn, it had found its way to Sotheby's decades later. Walter, heir to the vast Haverstone aluminum empire, had acquired it and its provenance three years ago for his private collection at Stonegate, the family's estate near Mt. Evans. At Walter's suggestion and the direction of the curator, the masterpieces were rotated from time to time for restoration or cleaning.

When the Haverstone family had sought expert help, they'd turned to Arabella. Leo was dating Willow Haverstone at the time. She was Walter and Ruth's only daughter. Leo had told Arabella it was Willow who'd suggested over lunch that his sister might be a good choice to make the trusted repairs. Apparently, other names were dropped as well, like Yves St. Vrain, the in-house curator. Yet, Leo further shared that Willow's idea took hold.

It came as no surprise to Arabella that Walter had investigated her credentials and told her so. Soon after, in late November, he had personally called her to meet him at Stonegate to view the work, which had gone smoothly.

Arabella frowned at the driver who said, "Where do you want it dropped?"

Dropped? She shuddered at the thought. Along with her fine-tuned cleaning knowledge of painted surfaces and pigments, Arabella was good at giving directions.

"Gently, please. Ever so carefully," she urged. "Come with me inside. We can use the elevator." Old and creaky, it had once been used to move ice. It opened at the end of the hall on the second floor. "Follow me," she said, and they walked through the doorway to her studio.

"Now, good. Over there. On my work table. Centered, please."

The driver and the helper deftly unpacked the oversized bundle and placed it exactly where and how she needed it. Monet's masterpiece lay face-up on top of her waist-high, green felt-covered worktable under assorted overhead lights. She side-stepped the small wheeled cart with drawers that held the trusted tools of her trade.

Using a remote, Arabella quickly positioned a video camera to fill its lens with the whole spread of the canvas. She would turn it on when she began to work. A host of art history and student interns would learn from it, here and abroad.

Minutes later, the couriers left her alone. But when one kept company with Monet, one never felt alone. Approaching her work table, she could see the paint surface gently reflecting its colors and light. It almost shimmered like the surface of a hot desert road and rose up to greet her. She leaned in closer and adjusted her scarf so its purple tip would not touch the surface.

Donning a head lamp and blue surgical gloves, she settled on the stool she'd had made to fit her comfortable sitting position. Jars, tubes, misters, cotton balls and pads stood by ready. Arabella studied the canvas surface section by section. Awed with the brushstrokes, she made mental and paper notes. Years of study in New York and Italy learning the nature of the oil paints and varnishes of the time of impressionists helped her decide what solutions to apply and how to swipe away dust, soot, and other surface accretions.

Working in small areas was best. Merely touching an artist's brushstrokes connected her to an artist in a personal way. Finally, finally, she was closer to Monet! She exhaled to relax and increase control in her fingers. She applied a bit of pressure here and, with lighter swipes or rubbing, there for effective cleaning. Doing her work, she could almost sense Monet's hand guiding hers to bring out the best of his passion. It was an honor—always—an honor to work on a masterpiece.

So much so, Arabella couldn't keep it to herself. James Boyd had become her new boyfriend during the last few months. They clicked on every level, and admittedly she was falling for him. He'd been a trusted gallerist for fifteen years and knew art inside and out. Surely, he'd love to see the Monet so up close and personal. Take photos, even.

Stepping over to her desk, she reached for her cell phone and called him. When his voice mail kicked in, she said cheerily, "G'morning, sweet James. I have the Monet! Come see?"

She smiled with anticipation and put down the phone. Her mouth was going dry from excitement and she got a drink of water from the small but adequate kitchen.

Ready to work, Arabella returned to her work table. Time seemed to disappear. So deep into her zone of happiness for untold minutes, Arabella barely heard the footstep behind her. She half listened for another, but none had come. Focused on her next swipe with a cotton swab directly onto the blue paint, she soon reached for her fine tweezers and extracted a loose micro-chip next to a pinpoint of exposed canvas near Monet's signature. The chip would be visually verified and color matched for filling in the micro-dot.

"Cobalt," she guessed aloud as she placed the chip under a special scope for pigment composition and confirmation. Meanwhile, she let the color fill her heart and mood. Monet's intention, for sure.

His magical impressionism drew her in deeper for another moment. It was a sort of hypnotic escapism, she supposed. The battle for more storage space with Eugene Ketchum, the building owner, took a back seat. The hassles with her ex-boyfriend abandoned her. Her recent computer glitches turned trivial. Even her constant yearning to return to Italy for fun and more field work was fading.

This was a moment...

The chime of her grandmother's clock she'd inherited brought Arabella back with a full shake. She leaned toward the microscope and checked the analysis screen. It had finished analyzing the three characteristics of color according to Albert Munsell, who had developed a widely-accepted system of color notation: Hue, value, and chroma. Further testing of the chip would reveal pigment particles, finishes, texture, hardness, gloss, opacity, and solubility.

Arabella raised her eyebrows at the results. She was an expert in blue hues.

"Sapphire?" she murmured with surprise and shook her head. So unexpected...

"Are you sure?" came from behind her.

Stunned, Arabella swiveled around. His was the last voice she wanted to hear. "What're you doing here?"

He stepped to her side. "Thought you might be missing me."

She sighed. "Not in the least. We have nothing to say to each other. Please leave."

Her visitor smirked and dropped a sizable stack of loose cash on the table.

"What's that for?" Arabella raised her chin and asked icily.

"You'll figure it out, I'm sure." He ran a forefinger through her scarf.

"So, answer me. Are you sure it's sapphire?"

"It's unlikely. Monet favored cobalt blue." She nodded at the scope. "Must be a glitch."

Now the scarf lay firmly in his hands. Menacing fire blazed in his eyes.

"Take the money now."

"No. Stand back," she said, her voice wavering. "And take your stash with you. I don't want anything to do with whatever it is you have in mind."

He tilted his head to one side and looked almost apologetic.

"Hey, relax. Give me a minute, okay?"

She stiffened. "What for?"

"This..."

Before her next blink, the intruder swiftly stepped to her back and yanked the silk tightly around her neck...and yanked sharply. Arabella let out a reflexive hoarse scream. She tugged on the scarf with one hand to stop the pressure squeezing the life out of her—literally. Her eyes widened beyond wide, and she flailed her arms and lost her balance. She squeezed the edge of the worktable with her hand to gain purchase against her attacker. She knocked the cash into the air. Paint tubes and brushes scattered across the table.

Groans and gurgles met their end in her throat. Monet's colors and paint tubes swirled in front of her eyes. Dizzily, she grabbed a tube and squeezed so hard the top popped off. The pigment oozed into her palm as she slapped it down on the table next to the painting.

Every second released terror through her; perspiration stung her eyes. Weakening, she slumped over the Monet. Her face pressed against a pink water lily as darkness rose behind her eyelids. Arabella's senses sank down into cottony darkness...darker than cobalt blue, which soared into black. After a last single, slow-to-come heartbeat, Arabella Laurens felt herself slip away—quickly, and as dead as Monet.

One

Aunt Meredith Calls
Atlantic Beach, Florida

Diane Phipps, P.I., listened again to the message from Tom's Aunt Meredith, who lived in Denver. Her aging voice wavered as she spoke.

"Hi, Tom and Diane. Oh my, I've missed you again. Anyway, it's hard to believe that a whole year has passed since you'd visited me. When I drive by the art museum, I think of the good time we had at the Monet exhibit." Her tone deepened with concern while Diane sank into her yellow chintz chair where clients often sat when they came to see her.

"I'm calling...because something dreadful has happened." She paused. *"Do you remember the private reception at Stonegate after we left the museum? How we'd met Walter and Ruth Haverstone and their daughter Willow? You'd also met Yves St. Vrain, the curator for the family's private fine art collection. He'd showed all of us around.*

9

"Well, Yves and I go way back...we had even dated at DU." A bit of giggle, then, *"We still chat from time to time. Yves seems to have a lot on his mind, and..."* Again, a pause. *"Well, news travels fast through the Front Range Art Association. He just told me that Arabella Laurens was found murdered. Dreadful. She was quite a noted art restorer in Manitou Springs. She was working on that beautiful Monet from Walter's private collection when it happened.*

"Aside from the obvious, Yves is upset because the painting was under his care as Walter's curator. And if the murder wasn't enough, the Monet painting is part of a crime scene and will be kept for God knows how long. Who would do such a thing to that woman? Everyone is distraught, and Yves said he's having trouble sleeping." She broke for a cough. *"I worry for him... and you know how I don't like bad things happening to good people. Walter Haverstone wants answers and some extra help. So...I'm wondering if you would consider...Oh, drat. There goes my door bell. Call me, okay? Love you both."*

Diane dropped the cell phone onto her desk in her office. Shaking her head, she looked up as Tom ambled in the front door. He'd just come from a walk on Jax Beach. His Tommy Bahama shirt with soaring sail fish on it hung half open and nearly covering his khaki shorts. His flip flops tapped the wood floor while he made his way to her.

"Hey, honey, what's going on? When I left, you looked content and happy for a new day."

"We need to call your Aunt Meredith," she said, tensing up. She picked up the cell phone and handed it to her husband.

"Uh oh...Is she okay?"

She smiled up at him. "Just listen..."

Tom hit voicemail. In seconds his face contorted into a frown.

"She's upset. She wants help." Tom pointed the phone at her. *"Your* help."

Diane met his gaze dead on. "It seems so." Admittedly, the prospect intrigued her.

Tom raised his eyebrows. "I *know* so."

No further discussion was needed, except this from Tom. "I'm out again on assignment in two days. You just go. I'll catch up with you and Aunt Merrie later."

"Hmm-hmm." She boosted herself up into a sitting position with her legs crisscrossed. "Well, I *am* between cases right now."

"Not for long, dear. A fresh one's in Colorado waiting for you and your special touch." He nodded and winked.

She hedged. "I don't know anyone in Manitou Springs, and I just can't barge into a case. I need to be hired."

He nodded and waved the phone at her. "Walter Haverstone will hire you. Aunt Meredith said as much. I'm calling her back now."

Diane's heart thumped with anticipation. She'd often met interesting people in her line of private investigation. Walter Haverstone, a striking gray-haired man with understated style, stuck out from the crowd. She and Tom had spent merely an hour with him and his wife Ruth during the reception. They'd left her feeling good about wealthy people supporting the arts. Offering scholarships, buying fine art and sculpture, setting up galleries and the like. Hosting receptions, retreats, and speakers were part of the Haverstone family contributions.

As Diane remembered, Walter wasn't an artist, but he understood the experience of having personal moments with breathtaking masterpieces. He valued the effects of laying three-dimensional life on one-dimensional canvas. To him, his collection rang up way more than investment dollars and cents. Brushstrokes by masters fed his spirit. He lived *with* art and needed the soothing rush a painting offered.

She could only imagine how devastated Walter could become over the Monet being retained. It'd be akin to losing a child. Certainly, he'd want it back...with a vengeance. In this, she supposed they were alike. With her mighty, anti-crime heart, she wanted the crime solved.

Two

From Beach to Mountains

Two days later, after staying with Aunt Meredith, Diane rented a car in Denver. She drove south in threatening weather on I-25 past Castle Rock and through Monument to Colorado Springs. Admiring the views of Pikes Peak that crowned the city, she turned west on Hwy 24 to Manitou Springs.

Used to Florida flatness at sea level, she held the steering wheel firmly and focused on the steeper, winding road that took her higher and higher. The forested hills and reddish rocks seemed to swallow her up, yet she kept her foot steady on the gas pedal. She was on a new mission—a new case—another chance to even the score between good and bad.

Using her GPS, finding her lodging was easy enough. On Columbine Path, the small private one-story home was a rental that Aunt Meredith helped her secure from a friend. Charming, half way up a steep hill from Manitou Avenue, the pale blue wood frame place with white trim was idyllic and typical of the area. A short picket fence hemmed in the small front yard.

Street parking was in front with a sign posted that read: *Space saved for 3915. Thank you.* A narrow, worn brick walkway led past a leafy flower bed to a low raised front porch. The place had an air about it as if it were waiting to come back to life after a snowy winter.

Diane let herself in the front door with the key the owner had left under a clay pot. Taking a quick stock of the residence, she relaxed. She could work here easily enough. Except she'd be away from home... and Tom.

Bless him. He'd been royally gallant about all this. It had never been her goal to render investigative services cross-country. Still, if she could help solve a crime, he assured her she *should*. Besides, Aunt Meredith counted for a lot to Tom, and Diane had come to like her most for her hospitality and sincerity. Years ago, she'd taken him in over a summer while his parents sorted out their differences.

While Diane unpacked her bags in the small bedroom at the rear with its corner windows, her thoughts turned toward the reason she was there at all. *Murder.* The unsolved case was still an empty canvas to her. Facts were her paint to put together a harrowing picture. She wasn't an artist, but could cut and paste pretty well.

She'd brought two basic tools with her: a small white board for making notes, listing names, and hanging lines for links, and a cork board for pinning items, photos, notes, and sketches. They would temporarily replace her large case board back home. So far, she had no images to post.

However, a dead body existed. Means were named: death by strangulation. No rope burns or cord stripes. No wire cuts. Necktie was a possible weapon, but later named as a silk scarf. An approximate time of death declared, already three months ago. The crime scene was still under lockdown, a loft apartment converted to a studio in an historical mountain town.

In her introductory phone call yesterday to Detective Roger McGuire, she'd learned there was no apprehended suspect. A few people of interest were interviewed and dismissed. No clear motive had surfaced yet. No false alibis. No witnesses. No rewards for information.

Diane was looking at a totally clean slate, so to speak.

There was *also* a painting involved. A Monet, for heaven's sake, pointing to a possible motive? So maybe Arabella Lauren's death wasn't so mysterious? Kill the girl, steal the painting?

Logic slipped from Diane's mouth. "Except why was the painting left behind and not stolen?" The chance was ripe for grand theft. Why not use it? Then she was investigating a homicide. But nothing ever seemed *that* cut and dried.

Experience had shown her that the underbelly of cases bore wounds or scars. Reasons to hate and destroy festered and hid in the dark. There were layers to explore. Rough edges existed—deep down connections to make, and secrets to uncover. They often yielded pat evidence strong enough to hold up in court.

Diane itched to find them. There was no time like the present to get started. The workings went on in her head while she left the house on foot and trekked down the hill, taking in the small neighborhood as she went. Hanging a left, she headed west on Manitou Avenue and soon spotted police cars parked in the lot out front of the department further up on the right.

Meeting Detective Roger McGuire was tops on her appointment list. She'd come with a good recommendation from Detective Beau Brooks from the Duval County Sheriff's office back in Jacksonville Beach. She still expected that her role would be considered auxiliary, if invited at all.

McGuire met her at the front door. Middle-aged, with inquisitive hazel eyes with crinkles at the corners and slow to smile, he stood at about five feet ten inches; he also fit the dark blue uniform well. With God's grace, she passed his visual assessment of her and he led her into his office.

"Good to meet you," he said, and proffered his hand for a shake, which she accepted.

"Same. I'm here regarding the Arabella Laurens case, to do what I can to help solve it."

He sank into the chair behind his small desk. Everything in here is small, she thought. Except him.

"Your reputation has preceded you," he commented.

"Yes, Detective. Thanks to—"

"Beau Brooks. We met each other a year ago in Denver. Terrorism consults."

She nodded and sat where he pointed. "Yes, he was pleased with the outcome of a case back home where a mermaid was killed."

Detective McGuire crossed his arms and leaned forward on his desk. "No mermaids here, ma'am," he said, referring to her last case in Florida. "But...we do have a sticky homicide on our hands here in Manitou Springs."

Diane smiled. "Why's it sticky?"

McGuire threw up his hands. "No arrest, and folks around here want it settled. Our chief is catching pressure."

"Which rolls downhill," she said, meeting his wavering gaze with understanding.

"The victim was local and liked a lot, and we're moving too slow, or so it seems, according to the mayor. We're a small department, about twenty on the force to handle around ten thousand calls a year. Fifty-two hundred residents live here in about three-square miles. Some rough terrain in these parts. Sgt. Pete Woodrow...he's with the El Paso County Sheriff's Office...and I are partnered up and scratching deep."

Diane unbuttoned her coat. She liked his straight-on approach. "Do you have any coffee?"

He shrugged. "Not a damned drop. Ran out last night."

Now that hurt. "Oh."

"See that board over there?" he said.

No way to miss it. Large, gray, and full of markings.

"We were up to until three this morning again working this case."

"Anything new to come out of it?" she ventured.

"Nope. Do I look happy?"

"Nope." Diane raised her hand. "Am I to take this as an invitation to join the team?"

He rolled his fingers on the desk top and nodded slowly. "To a point."

She had half expected his reticence. Even so, eagerness ran through her. "Good, because I'm not wearing a uniform. I work independently but check in often. I have lots of questions and things to do to get started, including seeing the crime scene."

McGuire's phone rang. "Hold on," he told her. "Yes, Chief. She's here. Well, I..."

Diane shifted her gaze to the board the detective had indicated. Green marker was used for names, red for places and times. Lots of extra scribbling, too. And bountiful question marks. She hoped to add her findings to her own board back up at the rental house. In blue.

McGuire hung up and gave her a long look. "I don't know whether you are a Godsend or not, but—"

"I prefer to hope so," she interjected.

"...but you've been given *carte blanche*, lady. Someone cares a lot about this case."

"No more than I will."

This she believed. "I know the owner of the Monet. He's deeply upset. A woman died while cleaning his painting." Walter Haverstone was indeed paying Diane's tab. He wanted answers ASAP, and his investment back. Perhaps he'd had a chat with the chief?

Diane tilted her head. "I'd like to visit the crime scene, please. Check some files?"

Roger nodded. "Meet me at fifteen hundred, outside. We'll walk. The victim's studio is a couple of blocks away."

Pleased, she nodded. "Thank you. Sounds close."

He chuckled. "Everything here is close."

"The murderer might be, too."

He shook his head. "If so, he's a crusty bastard." He raised a warning finger. "Don't touch anything at the scene. Forensics *still* visits there."

"Evidence?"

"What they found has been transported to their lab in Springs. Last stop for the items: Here, under my direction."

Humor hit her. "You'll be storing a Monet in your garage? Would love to see it."

He smirked. "This is classified, Ms. Phipps. Its safekeeping will be entrusted to James Boyd. He's an established local gallerist and has lots of insurance and a good vault. His background check cleared."

Diane nodded. "Good choice, I'd say. One more question for now. Who last saw Arabella Laurens alive?"

"Other than her murderer, we believe it was the delivery men who brought her the painting." He stood. "Their electronic checkpoint delivery log is valid, and we found a signed off delivery receipt on her desk. It's in Evidence. The victim made a call after they left."

Already Diane's brain lit up. "To whom?"

"James Boyd. He found her. Dead as a dormouse. He's her boyfriend."

McGuire turned off his desk lamp.

Diane blinked. "But, what if he—?"

"Boyd's alibi is solid. He was at the vet up on the road a piece with his dog at her time of death. You see, Ms. Phipps? We've had a pressing situation on our hands...for three full months."

Three

Crime Scene Visit

Diane followed Detective McGuire as he let them into Arabella Lauren's studio.

"Be a good girl, don't mess with anything," he reminded flatly. "This was her world."

A six-panel folding screen created a false wall on the left of the rectangular room. It separated a casual day area of the loft from her studio, not a fully organized apartment. Her work area featured high ceilings, exposed brick walls and wide-planked wood floor. Charming, historic, and warm. Artful in its own right. Three tall, narrow arched boxed windows loomed ahead facing the front of the building. Wide sills were home to various plants, including a host of red geraniums in clay pots.

The walls were covered with art. A lot of mountain scenes and local wildlife. Colorful and original, it seemed to Diane. Arabella had supported the local art community, which certainly must have endeared her to them. Close-up photos of flowers and creeks, too, claimed space on the front wall between the windows. A few photos were of her, alone and with others. Hand-printed cards under each. *Arabella, Guest of Honor, Front Range Art Society Convention, Colorado Springs.* More photos were scattered about; one with her holding a shiny statue...*Milan, Outstanding Achievement Award ~ Renoir Restoration.*

"No wonder Walter Haverstone chose Arabella," Diane said to herself. Then she spotted a news article from the local *Pikes Peak Bulletin*: Fine Art Restoration Studio Opens.

Awed at the array of other commendations, Diane raised her cell phone and snapped pictures to study them later.

"Here," McGuire said. "You'll need these." He handed her a file folder. "The victim was found right there, slumped over the end of the worktable. She fell forward with the left side of her head planted on top of the painting she was working on." He walked over to the wall and flipped on a light switch.

Diane stepped further inside and eyed the victim's setup for work.

"She was right-handed."

McGuire watched her. "Right-handed, yes. Explains the paint in her right hand."

"The victim chose the narrow end of the table from which to work with the painting undoubtedly laid out with the top up there and the bottom in front of her. So, the Monet is a vertical painting, not horizontal."

"Correct, Ms. Phipps."

"Hmm. A bit different."

"How so?" he asked, curious.

"I think many of his canvases are horizontal, that's all."

McGuire added, "This one was covered in water lilies." His intense expression softened somewhat. "Pretty."

It impressed her that he could temporarily slip into an appreciative mode. "Different can be more valuable," she commented.

Diane then trained her gaze over almost everything. "Her microscope looks expensive and sophisticated. High powered, too. For paint analysis?"

"Like I said, I don't know much about art. But she had the reputation of fixing up cracks better than a welder. Seamless. Undetectable. An expert in saving art."

Diane mused aloud. "It'd been nice to have met her."

"Too late..." He dropped his gaze. "Sorry."

She frowned. "Anything in particular your team found in here?"

The detective nodded. "Three brand-new one hundred-dollar bills. One in the trash. One underneath the radiator over there." It was the old kind of radiator made of iron, painted white, and used for radiant heat. "Another one up on that shelf."

She gazed at the different places, wide apart from one another. "Hmm. The bills were scattered. Yes, interesting. Anything else?"

"Two forensic teams have been over this place. It's more like what they didn't find. No clear footprints, no drugs, no fingerprint—to date—except hers. No murder weapon, no clues from the makeshift kitchen, or the bathroom, except for the open window in the little storage room. Killer didn't make himself coffee and hang out here long. No clothes found, either."

She figured aloud, "No time to spare for a getaway. He was on a mission and sought her out. Anyone see someone coming or going?"

"Nobody saw anybody, coming or going. Not much traffic in these back alleys."

She pressed on. "How about the ME report?"

"Death by strangulation. Neck wounds and bruises. Broken esophagus."

"Anything under her fingernails?"

"Green felt and traces of denim. She was wearing jeans."

"Hair or skin?"

"Still in forensics."

Diane glanced at him with disbelief. "For three months? Jeepers," she murmured under her breath.

"It's not my shop," he groused.

Point taken. Evidence, depending on its nature, got sent all over the country for analysis. Not to mention mistakes in returning reports that took time to sort out.

Diane next slid her gaze from left to right. The layout of the room made sense. If only the walls could talk. She walked closer to the table and noted the tools of Arabella's trade.

Using her senses, she tried to soak up how the space *felt,* hoping for something unusual to rise. Crime scenes told stories and murderers often left calling cards. Trite, but true. She just had to be sensitive enough to spot them. She was doing her best. These detectives needed a break.

What looked to be an overhead camera mounting caught her attention.

"Arabella filmed her work?"

He nodded. "Only thing on the recorder was the painting. Five seconds worth. Turned on, turned off."

Diane looked down at the green felt covering the table. A smattering of paint and part of a handprint darkened the short end of the table where the victim had been found.

"What's this?" she asked, pointing without touching.

"Evidence of a struggle," McGuire said. "She almost twisted herself out of her boots."

Diane bent down to eye level. The felt on the table was scratched. Thus, green fibers under her nails.

"Anything else of consequence from the ME?"

"Just the oil paint smeared in her right hand and some dried coffee creamer on the other."

Diane looked over at the array of pigments strewn next to some loose brushes and cotton swabs. Little bottles of solutions and a blow dryer. It suddenly all seemed so personal. She was standing in the space of a person's death. She winced. She was trying to be logical, factual, taking cues from what was in front of her. She blocked her imagination in order to not distort what had happened and how.

"That stool is just how it was left, fallen over?" she asked, trying not to get caught in a leg.

"Everything here is, except for portable evidence. Like her cell phone. The cash. The video camera tape. Trash container. The paint tube. Beyond that, her bank account showed nothing weird. Nor does her cell phone. The list is in that folder," McGuire said, cutting into the silence.

Diane put her hands on her hips. "So...how'd the killer get in?"

He gestured to his right. "The window in the storage room was found open. Fire escape out there. It was colder here then. It was unlikely she had opened it for fresh air."

She strode over to where he gestured and entered the room. The shelves were in good order. Cleaning supplies and some non-perishable food items and bags of potting soil took up the space on them. The window was closed, of course, and the pane a bit hazy. She leaned toward it and gazed down to the side alley below.

"May I stay a while?" she called out to the detective and went back out into the main room. She was eager to go over the place with her own fine-toothed comb.

He cleared his throat. "It's not suggested."

Unsurprised, she figured asking was worth a shot. She had a way to go to gain these officers' trust to truly give her free range.

"So, what guy would want to kill her?"

He paused and raised a finger. "How'd you know it was a guy who did the job?"

Diane smiled. "No lady I know can pull down one of those old heavy iron fire escapes to climb up onto. And that one's rusty. Bet it even creaks."

McGuire squinted at her. A glimmer of admiration popped up, but quickly retreated. Seemingly, a man of limited praise. Short of cynicism, it could get like that in this business.

"Don't know," he said. "This scene is still how we found it, except for some new dust that's accumulated since lockdown. But her friend said Arabella often did her work listening to classical music. Loudly. She probably didn't hear a creak or footsteps. Guy took her by surprise."

That seemed classic for an attack from behind. "May I ask what friend?"

"Ask away," he said. "Her name's Pam Piper. She's good people. Father owns the hardware store."

"I'd like to meet her. Where is she?"

Diane still had so much to learn about the victim. Good friends often shared meaningful things, secrets even that turned into sound leads. Maybe Pam had a few to share?

"Not far," McGuire answered.

Diane laughed. "Really?" slipped out with some sarcasm.

He sighed. "Her jewelry shop's right across the street. Piper's Treasures." He continued, "They were close and supposed to have lunch that day."

Before Diane walked to the front windows for a look, she gazed down at the floor by her feet. "Hmm. Is this a partial print here? Rust is my guess, not dust. Has it been processed?"

"Yes."

"And?"

"Inconclusive. Notice, there are plants on the landing. They were hers and needed watering. Partial print is probably hers from taking care of them out there."

Diane raised her chin. "Possibly, except they're still wintering in non-freeze pots, Detective."

She turned on her heel and pointed to another feature in the room. "Where does that dumbwaiter go?"

He swiveled in that direction. "First floor. This whole second floor was once a private gentlemen's club. Fancy, meals, cards, and... entertainment. Kitchen was downstairs. Now it's Frankie's Bakery. I'm sure you noticed."

She did, actually. The aromas streaming out of there would trip up any devoted dieter. "I plan to stop in later. Does it work?"

"Absolutely. Very popular shop here in town. A mom and pop place."

She listened with interest. Recommendations would help her get settled, even if it were only for a short while. "I meant the dumbwaiter.

Does the dumbwaiter work?" she said. "Means of arrival or escape...for a man...or a woman?"

McGuire moved toward the door and dutifully recited, "A *dude* killed her, not a lady."

Diane walked over to the dumbwaiter and lifted the stainless cover. She peered inside the gaping shadow. There was nothing but a brick cavity and exposed ropes on the sides. A dark steel plate shelf waited below.

"Have you seen it in operation?"

"Only from downstairs. It groans. Two shelves, close together, Ms. Phipps, meant for delivery of pastries, hot soup for lunch, not Lilliputian murderers."

Diane smirked wryly. "Well, that's no fun."

He handed her a hard look. "None of this is. The dumbwaiter was where the murder weapon was found." He gestured for her to leave with him. "Can we wrap this up? Are you finished?"

Diane buttoned up her humor and pocketed her phone. Levity had no effect on McGuire. But it did help her. The afternoon was almost over, and she'd hardly cracked a smile the whole time. She was only recently learning to inject a few wild hare thoughts into the seriousness of what she did for a living. She rationalized that it was about maintaining balance of the psyche.

All work in crime investigation and no play make Jack a dull boy—or push him down into a rabbit hole of nothing but grim details piled high and deep to keep him company. She cringed at the thought.

Thankfully, Tom understood her need for comic relief, bless him. He laughed at every one of her campy, crappy jokes. It'd been three days since they'd parted. By then he was headed out to his new classified surveillance assignment. He'd hinted Montana, for another indefinite time.

Renegade militia is misbehaving. Tom had his own version of rabbit holes. But his were far more dangerous than ferreting out a slug who had killed an art restorer. She hoped for a text from him tonight.

Chilly, Diane stuffed her hands into her jacket pocket. The heat had been turned off. She needed to buy mittens and a scarf, and to meet Pam Piper. It could be pleasant. She loved jewelry.

Four

Getting to Know You

The next morning Diane left the rental house, again by foot. Walking around there was the way to go. She stopped by Frankie's Bakery, and aside from the glass domes hoarding stacks of donuts on the counter, the tin ceiling caught her eye. Everything up there possessed character. She glimpsed the dumbwaiter off to the left where she could also see into the kitchen. Patrons lingered and chatted around her.

"Hi," one woman, about fifty, dressed in a smart wool pea coat and hat said to her. "You're the private investigator, right? I saw you unloading your car yesterday. Forgive me for not stopping by then, but you looked pretty busy. I'm Marie. Your neighbor."

Diane returned her smile. "Yes, I'm here on a visit. Nice to meet you. I'll probably be in and out a lot."

Marie shook her head. "Well, I'm hoping you can make some sense out of what happened to that poor woman. It's hard resting at night knowing a killer is on the loose around here. We're a small community, and we look after each other best we can. Come over for coffee when you can. I know Arabella's boyfriend, James. I buy art from him."

Diane regarded her quietly for a moment. "I'll make a point to come over. Soon. Until then, did they seem a happy couple?"

"Better than most. They met not very long ago...in November."

Diane pointed to a glazed donut with sprinkles for the counter clerk.

"So, they were pretty much a new item?"

"Good case for love at first sight, I'd say," Marie assured her. "How come you don't have a scarf and mittens? You'll catch a cold faster than grease lightning hittin' the Peak."

"I'm working on it. Any suggestions where to find them?"

Maria hooked her thumb over her shoulder. "Two doors up. Geneva's for Women. I gave up knitting long ago, or I'd make you some."

Diane ordered a coffee, too. "That's very kind of you."

Maria shrugged. "Glad to help the lady who's going to settle this mess." There wasn't a shred of doubt in her blue eyes. Her sentiment filled Diane with gratitude...and apprehension. Law enforcement was doing its best. She'd do her job, too, and she wasn't here to outshine them. But fresh eyes helped, more often than not. She could catch something crucial. It might take a while. But one thing for sure, she wasn't a quitter.

A half hour later, Diane sat with Pam Piper. The jewelry maker was about thirty-five. Her dark hair was pulled back into a loose chignon at the nape of her neck. Her Bohemian shirt looked hand-woven. Its beaded hem fell casually over loose beige linen pants.

Diane introduced herself, and said, "I'm here to talk about Arabella. I understand you were friends?"

Pam's brown eyes saddened. "Yes. I so miss her...I just saw her the evening before...well, before...you know...before she was..." Her chin quivered. "I can't even say the word."

Diane had read Detective McGuire's notes early that morning. Pam's statement to the police was short but as heartfelt as Diane was observing her to be now. "We're trying to get to the bottom of this," she began. "I need your help."

Pam nodded slowly and waved for Diane to follow her into a little office where they resettled on folding chairs in front of a low worktable. Strands and tubes of colored beads, rolls of colored cord, copper wire, and small boxes of gold and silver clasps claimed the back part of the table beneath little cubicles above what looked like mini-mailboxes.

"What do you need me to do?" Pam asked.

Diane pulled a notepad and a pen from her purse. "I didn't know the victim. I just need you to talk about her. Tell me whatever comes to mind."

Pam took the cue with grace. "Ara and I met shortly after I opened my shop last year. We usually had lunch on Tuesdays. She talked a lot about her work...she'd studied with the best, as far as I could tell. We both had our businesses to tend to, but we kept an open door for each other. We could even wave to each other from our windows. Sometimes, if business was slow in here, I'd cross the street and go up to see her and hang out for a while." She reached for bottled water and sipped. Then, she rubbed the worry stone pendant she wore. Diane couldn't help notice its beauty. "That's quite pretty," she said about the solid copper teardrop.

Pam lifted it toward her. Diane could see her reflection in the polished surface.

"Thanks. I made it in memory of Arabella. I wear it most days. It's called "Yesterday."

"Nice. Was she a happy person?" Diane asked.

"Up and down, really. And when she was hired to clean the Monet, she was very excited and content. I think meeting James helped a lot with stabilizing her feelings. They'd met out on the pavement on Manitou Avenue. She wanted her picture taken with the carved bears in front of the Two Bears shop. It's a photo hotspot. He obliged, and that's what got things going. They went together to the Christmas Ball.

He dressed as a woodsman, and she wore a winter fairy gown...with a faux fur cloak. Gorgeous. They'd made a stunning couple. I don't know if he'll ever be the same." She paused. "Ara deserved his goodness, more than most, I'd say."

Diane nodded. "Why's that?"

"Ara's love life was rocky for a while. Sam Crawford turned out to be a disappointment." Her voice was terse.

"Sam Crawford?"

"Yeah, the guy she was going with before James came along. James was her salvation. He helped put her heart pieces back together. I never did like Sam much, but Arabella had trouble seeing him for who he really was. A cheat. He bought an expensive, original necklace from me, a large fire opal with gold wire. I thought it was for Ara, but nope.

"Two weeks later I was in Miramont Castle and saw Susan Watson wearing it. She's a tour guide. I admired how it looked on her, and she said it was a gift...from her new guy. Blew me away, I'll say."

"Would've bothered me, too," Diane remarked.

"Sam's really good-looking, but it all stops there. Not one for commitment. Ara wanted to break it off, but he kept coming around. Made it hard on her. Wasn't very nice, really. I even saw him briefly the morning she died. He was passing by out front right after I had opened. He stalled out for a bit."

Diane looked up from her notes. "Was he window shopping?"

Pam frowned. "It seemed to me he was looking up at Arabella's studio. He finished his coffee, threw the cup in the bin, and moved on."

"Moved on to where?"

"Most likely up the hill to the brokerage office he owns. Real estate. Expensive real estate, takes him away from time to time, even abroad."

Diane noted that, too. "So, James is a gallerist?"

Pam brightened. "Now, he's a stand-up guy, the best. Winner of our Local Best Business Award for two years in a row. He knows a ton about art, has an incredible library of art books, keeps up his place, and helps his patrons get what they want. For a while, I had a thing for him. But when I met Ted, everything changed. We're getting married at Christmas." She wiggled her ring finger.

Diane wished her the best. "Did Arabella complain about anything? Share secrets? Did she have problems in her family?"

"Only girl secrets, like who was hot and who was not. Movies, fashion trends. No lasting feuds going on with her family. Except, she'd get into it with her brother sometimes...sibling rivalry." Pam brushed some crumbs from the worktable into a small trash can. "But Sam was a pesky thorn in her side. Ara was straight with him. While they were dating, he'd turn up late a lot, or not at all. More than once she had to pay their dinner bill. She grew tired of it and let him know it was over for her. Still, he'd leave notes on her studio door, text messages, and the like."

Diane raised an eyebrow. "A lot?"

Pam shifted positions in her chair. "Enough for her to finally say something to James about it. She was pretty independent, and it took a while because she gave the benefit of doubt too much. Anyway, Sam suddenly stopped with his antics."

Diane tapped the pen cap on her bottom lip. "Since you're right across the street, did you notice anything unusual that morning?"

"Unusual? Nope. I did see the delivery van pull out from the alley. It had turned left and stopped long enough to pick up one of the delivery guys coming out of Jake's Jerky Shop."

Diane listened. Pam had been through it with this, but her willingness to remember things that some folks wouldn't want to get close to again shone brightly.

"Do you like jerky?" Pam asked off-handedly. "It's dried up meats, chewy, spiced, and salty as heck."

Diane's taste buds gave their regrets. "Can't say I would."

"No loss, as far as I'm concerned, either. Cowboys like it enough, though. Anyway, that was that. I wanted to see the Monet so badly but waited for Arabella to call. She was a sharer and a giver by nature. She'd never keep anything so spectacular to herself. That morning, I had two clients and got into helping them. Next thing I know, the police drove up, and all heck broke loose. I called James at the gallery, but got his voice mail." Pam's shoulders slumped. "I had the most awful feeling of dread..."

~ * ~

That evening, Diane went over her notes and perused all the contents of Detective McGuire's file folder. The photos of the victim were graphic and an abbreviated medical examiner's report provided details. Approximate time of death was 10:30 a.m. She also checked the photocopy of the delivery sheet Arabella had signed with initials applied from the couriers. All seemed to be in order there.

But something extraordinary had happened not long after... someone literally squeezed the life out of Arabella. He knew where he could find her and how to get to her. In and out, unseen. The perp left no evidence of carrying a weapon. Instead, she was unwittingly wearing one. It was beautiful—silk and richly colored. Perhaps it'd been a special purchase or a gift from someone.

Also, it was highly unlikely that a total stranger had dropped in for the job. Diane suspected the victim knew her attacker. Broad-shouldered and strong enough to unfold the bottom of the fire escape and strangle a woman. Question was: What had tripped his switch to commit homicide? Diane sighed at her plight. Motives were the most elusive of elements.

Soon, Diane got ready for bed. The back bedroom was chilly, and she'd brought cotton pajamas--suitable for Florida nights. Pulling an old Northwestern University hoodie on for extra warmth, she adjusted the thermostat and climbed in between the flannel sheets.

Her mind rambled. She yearned to be able to run by what she'd learned today with Tom, except no call came through. She sincerely hoped he was thinking of her...and was warmer than she was.

Five

Meeting the Boyfriend

James Boyd wore round glasses, looked studious, and was thin in stature. His dark hair spilled over his forehead and brushed his eyebrows. He was good-looking, too, with a straight mouth. He looked comfortable in a thick, deep green sweater with bears and deer knitted into the sleeves that bulked up his appearance. Here was a man of refinement...mountain-style with polish. The color of his cord pants resembled the gray bark of a ponderosa pine, with hints of goldish rose in the soft threads. But his tan shirt was crisp and clean, and no tie needed. Keens wrapped his feet, ready for a hike at any time. Maybe they were part of the local dress code.

He stood out from the array of artwork mounted on the pale gray walls behind him. Overhead track lighting highlighted gilded, fancy frames and those of polished wood surrounding original works of an eclectic collection of paintings. The arrangement itself was a work of art. Sensitively and intelligently shown, each painting was set up to feature its best side, like a portrait.

It came as no surprise to Diane why Arabella had been drawn to him. Well-mannered, too. He'd invited her in immediately and poured her some coffee.

"She was the best woman I've ever met," James began, meeting Diane's gaze directly. "I will *never* understand why this happened... why the universe has given us this." His dark brown eyes teared up, undoubtedly for the thousandth time.

"I'm so sorry..." Diane murmured.

James lowered his head for a moment and struggled for composure.

"Look, I know the cops are doing their best." James settled on a stool by the front counter.

She nodded and hopped up onto the one next to him. "They are. The guy was lucky not to be seen."

"*Which* guy?" he spat.

"If we knew, he'd be locked up by now."

His coffee mug hit the counter harder than needed. Liquid sloshed out over the rim and ran dangerously close to a pile of his business cards. "Well, my money's still on that creep ex-boyfriend of hers, Sam Crawford. Some guys can't take rejection, you know? He failed in college. He got discharged from the Army, dishonorable. Lost jobs and now works for himself. A true, broken loser. What she ever saw in him—except for looks—I'll never know. Neither does Pam."

Diane thought for a minute. "Your Arabella was a restorer by trade. She had a lot of experience with resurrection and repairs. Maybe she thought she could fix him up, save him? Happens to women more than you think. An unfortunate trap, really."

James set his jaw firm. "He hit her, you know."

Diane widened her eyes. "No, I didn't."

"She told me, not Pam. After she broke it off with him, he kept bugging her. So I paid him a visit." He hesitated. "Not proud of it now, but somebody had to take care of this. So, I asked him to show me some property near the Incline. He drove me up, and then I decked the shit out of him once. Left him up there for bear bait and took the Barr Trail back down here."

Diane had a little trouble visualizing the event. James wasn't exactly Rambo. But she took him for his word. "Maybe that's why Crawford had stopped bothering her?"

"Probably not." He held up his hands. "I'm lousy with my fists, but I started ju-jitsu over at Corky's. I got a promo deal, and a guy like me needs a little help in a tight squeeze. It was enough to make my point with Sam."

"Good job," Diane said and threw him an irreverent high five.

"Nah, I think he stopped because he knew someone else was on to what he was doing to her. Serving time for assault gave him the jitters. The lily-livered coward."

Diane lifted her chin. Well, there it was. If *this* was how Sam Crawford operated, she could strike him off her suspect list. Murder would've sent him straight to a Xanax bottle. Unless...he mixed it with whiskey, then anything could've happened.

"Truly," Diane agreed. One thing murderers had in common was cowardice.

A moment of silence dropped.

"I heard you found her?" she said gently.

James straightened his spine and pushed his mug away. "She'd left me a voice message to come by and see it. Just like her to do that," he said ruefully. "She knew how much being mere inches away from those brushstrokes would have meant to me. But when I got there, she was...gone. Horribly gone. I could hardly punch nine-one-one on my phone. I felt gutted and was sitting on her couch when the police came. The window was open in the storage room, and that was strange. It was January 7th, and damned cold out." He stopped. "If it weren't for Degas, my dog, needing his shots, I'd have been there earlier. Might've made a difference."

Diane left him to work it through. Unfounded guilt could do such a number on people who knew victims well. "How'd you get in to her studio?"

"When I got there, I knocked, although she wouldn't have minded me walking in. But the door was locked. She was mindful of security because of her project. But she'd given me keys to her place and studio weeks before. We were getting closer all the time." He pulled out his Black Bear Diner key ring. "Used to be right here, between my shop key and my car key. But the cops have it now." He grimaced and tossed them down next to the mug. "Her life in that studio is all locked up now."

"It needs to be. Things can be overlooked."

James pointed to the large blooming plants on a wide shelf by the front window. "Those are her geraniums, which she loved. After Detective McGuire confirmed my alibi, for God's sake, he said, 'Take 'em. They've been processed.' But Ms. Phipps, her happy place is forever shut down..."

Diane relied on how people just opened up and talked to her. Even those who played their cards close to their chests opened up. It was some God-given trait of hers to listen neutrally, which came in handier than ever these days. She pushed forward. "How was her funeral?"

James drew up and briefly raised his eyes in memory. "Saddest one I'd ever been to, honestly. Saint Andrews was packed. The service was delayed for two days due to her parents getting caught in a blizzard south of Boulder. I was glad to meet them. They own a ski equipment company. Her brother Leo is a chemist for a pharm company and helps run a microbrewery on the side. He lives in upscale LoDo in Denver. He and his girlfriend, Willow Stonehaven, and I had beers and burgers together at The Keg after everyone left the cemetery. Willow was quiet, reserved. A horsewoman. Apparently, she'd first suggested Arabella do the work for the family."

"Rightfully so, as far as I can tell."

"Thank you. Leo and Willow came down later to clear out Arabella's apartment. I...I took some personal things back home. Turned my key over to the owner. They had to put some of her stuff in storage. They're coming back next week to pick it up. You might want to meet them?"

"I surely would." She was glad for the chance. Something beneficial for her investigation could come out of it. At least she could give her condolences.

"Good. We'll meet up then."

Arabella's apartment. Dismayed, Diane pursed her lips. She'd become so immersed in the crime scene, she'd failed to ask Detective McGuire about its condition. Surely, he'd written about her place in his notes, with which she needed to catch up later.

James cleared his throat. "I met other people in Arabella's life that day. The Walter Stonehaven clan came with some of his staffers at the estate. I'd never met Walter but had heard of his private collection through other art lovers at the Front Range Art Society. We spoke, also due to our mutual interests. He had a tough time at the funeral."

"I imagine so," Diane said thoughtfully. Imagine was all she could do now, really.

"Mr. Stonehaven's very concerned. He figures she was killed because she was working on an ultra-valuable masterpiece from his collection. 'Somebody wanted to steal that painting,' he'd told me. 'But they bungled job.' Maybe because of an interruption? Thing is, Walter's not a happy man over this, and his Monet is still in lock-up, Lord knows where."

Diane looked up from her notes. "It's at the forensics lab in Colorado Springs for now."

"A good place," he confirmed. "I know Morgan Newberry. He's a forensic art investigator and does some work for them. See, all is not pretty in the art world."

Diane wrote down the name and resumed, "Then I understand the painting will be delivered to you by Detective McGuire for safekeeping as evidence until the case is closed."

James's eyes brightened. He bowed slightly and crossed his hands over his chest. "It'll be my honor. Walter and I decided to meet again one day soon. I have a Charles Rockey, a noted local artist, he's interested in. Walter has a good eye. And a beautiful estate, Arabella said. He has horses, too. Lusitanos. Expensive and beautiful." He tipped his mug toward Diane. "If I were into ranching, which I'm not, it'd be for horses. Nothing prettier than horses running loose on the prairie," he added wistfully.

Diane finished writing. "I'm fond of them myself."

"Rydell Coburn, the guy who takes care of Walter's horses, came to pay his respects. He's the farrier...does blacksmithing and some home-bred security. He watches over the stock and fixes fences, too. I mentioned he ought to do a shoeing demo during our version of frontier days. Says he might. He visits occasionally; likes it here."

"Who wouldn't?" Diane said quickly. "I mean, you're living in a piece of heaven."

James smiled for the first time. "Also, I'd met Yves St. Vrain. He's the curator for the Stonegate art collection. Seems a fine enough man, knowledgeable, and about to retire. He's *really* bent. Said he's hung an empty frame where the Monet was displayed. Mrs. Haverstone added a black ribbon in mourning...missing their amazing art...and mourning a talented woman."

James choked out the last word. Tears came. "Sorry, it just hits me, and I lose it."

Diane fought the urge to hug him. This part of her work was never easy. "We've had enough for now, James. You've been a champ. We'll meet again. Here's my card. I'll be around."

The gallerist got up from the stool and showed her to the door.

"One more thing...on the positive side," he began. "I did get to see the Monet."

Diane smiled. "Light comes with the dark. And you will again. Up close and personal."

He hesitated. "There was so much in front of me. Arabella. Everything scattered. The radio playing Vivaldi. Water lilies, pink and rose colored, floating on blue water. Deliberate, short brushstrokes applied next to each other like stepping stones." He used his fingers to demonstrate. "Monet really was something, you know. So gifted. So memorable. Just won't leave my head."

Diane slowed at the door. The imagery even shook her.

"I need to go now," she said. "Anything comes up, call me. I'm up on Columbine Path."

"I heard."

She raised an eyebrow.

"It's a small community," James offered.

Diane, frustration rising, said, "Then you'd think somebody would've seen something that morning in the side alley."

Six

The Ex-Boyfriend

Diane went home and took a nap. She'd been feeling the need more than usual and chalked it up to altitude adjustment. Her cell phone ringing was what woke her. Tom's image filled the screen. It was one of him with his hair all ruffled from the beach breeze and the ocean stretching out behind him.

"Ohh, it's you..." Her tone grateful. "I miss you."

"How's it going?" Tom's familiar deep voice soothed her. No background noise came through.

She sighed. "It's beautiful here."

"Here, too."

"I had to buy a hat and mittens at Geneva's. Really nice shop; squeezed in some retail therapy."

He grunted approval. "Send me a pic. It's been a while since I've seen you bundled up for winter. I saw a moose this morning."

"Lucky you. Are you in the woods?"

"Sometimes. Snow's deep. How's the case...any progress?"

She sat up and pulled the covers higher. "I haven't met all the people I need to yet. But there are some good folks here. Helpful. Upset. But the victim made an enemy somewhere along the line. Cash was involved, too."

"A payoff?"

"I don't know who was paying whom, and whatever for, I have no idea...yet. Walter Haverstone is being generous. All my food tabs and gas are paid for. I'm eating out a lot and am walking everywhere instead of driving. I look at that Incline and get dizzy. It looks straight up. Detective McGuire said it's more than twenty-seven hundred steps to the top. Don't know how people make it."

Tom offered, "Step by step, I guess. Rests in between. I have a buddy who trained for it. He said it was the most strenuous thing he's ever done."

"I can believe." She fiddled with the edge of the quilt. "Anyway, pressure's on the force. My work's going slowly, but I'm trying not to miss anything. The woman never had a chance, Tom. It's sad."

He whistled. "You keep at it, dear. Something'll give, and you'll crack it wide open."

Diane's heart swelled. "Thanks, I needed that."

Tom added, "Meanwhile, take it step by step, okay? Not sure when I'll call again. We're on the move a lot."

Diane swallowed. His work with DeepSur2, the classified federal surveillance agency, had taken them from St. Louis to its new home base in Florida. His job often took him away from her. Worry would set in, and she had to handle home things by herself. *Her* work made him worry for her, as well. They'd accepted that this was part of their career territory. Together, they were united in fighting the good fight. She closed her eyes. She missed their closeness.

"I packed Twizzlers for you," she said quietly.

He chuckled. "I had one with breakfast. Thanks. Love you."

"Love you," she said softly, and he was gone.

~ * ~

Detective McGuire met Diane for coffee the next morning. This time he brought Sgt. Pete Woodrow with him, from the El Paso County Sheriff's office. He was dark-haired, fit, younger and shorter than McGuire, who clocked in at approximately forty-five years old. Pete had wanted to meet Diane.

"How's it going?" he asked her and shook her hand. It was a firm shake.

"I'm getting better oriented here, thanks. Meeting folks."

McGuire asked, "Anything new from Forensics?"

"Nada."

They both swigged their coffee in thought.

"I interviewed James Boyd," Diane said and added more cream to hers.

"What'd you think?"

"He needs closure to all this."

"We all damned do," McGuire said, as his radio went off. "Number six-five-o, report back to home office," the female dispatcher said. He shifted his weight on the stool and eyed Pete. He replied, "Purpose?"

"It's regarding the homicide. Sam Crawford's here. Wants to meet with you."

Diane's ears perked up at the sound of his name. She'd yet to meet Arabella's questionable ex-boyfriend.

"May I join you?" she asked politely, picking up her bag.

Both men swiveled their gazes to her in tandem. "Our pleasure," McGuire said.

"Wonder what it's about," Pete put in.

Diane walked with them to the front door and out on the pavement. "Maybe he's remembered something important," she said and tugged on the new knitted hat with a Nordic design she'd found at Geneva's. She had a hunch there was more to learn about him. Despite James Boyd's opinion of the guy, there were two sides to every story.

Twenty minutes later, Diane sat with the three men in a small office of the Manitou Police Department. Fluorescent lighting shone down on them and a grey table with no drawers. Very utilitarian, but the chair seats were padded in black cloth. She pulled out her notebook and pen and noted the time, date, and those present.

"What's on your mind, Sam?" Detective McGuire asked. Crossing his arms, he leaned back in the chair he'd chosen at the head of the table. *"A lot?"*

Sam tilted his head to one side, catching his drift. "Look, I had a memory flash. Wanted to drop it on you."

Pete shot him a hard gaze. "Like your real whereabouts the morning Arabella Laurens was murdered?"

Sam returned a steely glance. "I was solidly at my office. Dated e-mails with sent times proved it. My assistant Pauline confirmed my presence. We're past that now, and I—"

"We're not past anything," Detective McGuire stated, "until we find out who killed Ms. Laurens."

Diane raised her chin. Small group dynamics could be all cheery and happy, supportive. Yet, this small group severely lacked a social spark of the friendly kind. It was obvious these two had gone around and around before. She scrawled a note on her pad and passed it to McGuire. *Virtual assistant? Delayed auto-sent e-mail messages?"*

He shook his head from side to side briefly.

Dead end there. She settled back and let whatever was going to come out of this to happen.

"Fine," Sam said. "But if I'd killed her, I'd have skipped town long ago. But I didn't. I'm right *here*." He jabbed his forefinger down on the table top for emphasis. "And I have something to *report*."

McGuire acquiesced. "Then, get on with it, Mr. Crawford."

Sam leaned further toward the center of the table. "The morning Arabella died, I had walked to work like I usually do...when I'm in town. I was running a little late that day, but I'd stopped at Fred's for a takeout coffee."

"We know," Pete interjected flatly.

Sam narrowed his eyes at Pete. "I don't know why, maybe it's because I still missed Arabella—she's the kind of woman who's hard to forget—I slowed up out front of Pam Piper's shop and looked across the street and up at Arabella's studio."

Diane nearly cringed, remembering how James had relayed that Sam had hit Arabella. Feeling cynical, she guessed it was *hard* on Sam giving up his chance to take out his wrath on his girlfriend? That alone put him in a low-life category. How far down low it got was what had initiated police interrogation of Sam, who ended up having an alibi, as a person of interest.

"It was over between us, but it still would've been nice to catch of glimpse of her. Just for a few seconds, mind you. I had a tough time when she broke it off. Anyway, my alarm went off on my watch, which helps keep me on time, and I dumped my cup and walked on up the street."

Diane listened as he spoke. Her gut level told her Sam was on the level about all this. She glanced at McGuire and Woodrow, and nothing on their faces contradicted his accounting.

"Say, do you mind if I smoke?" Sam asked abruptly, and pulled a pack of Marlboro cigarettes from his shirt pocket.

"Yes," all chorused in unison.

He sighed and put them away again.

McGuire looked at his watch. "Listen, Sam, we're here to hear what you have to say."

"Right," Pete Woodrow said. "You called for this meeting, so let's have it."

Sam ran a finger over his eyebrow. "Yeah, about that," he began. "I've been seeing the announcements on TV about having any information to call in...Well, I came in."

McGuire just looked at him and waited.

"I don't know if it means anything, but..."

"But what?" Pete pushed.

Before Sam resumed, he slid Diane an apologetic look.

"I saw a guy taking a leak."

McGuire scowled and exchanged an unhappy glance with Woodrow. Detective McGuire widened his eyes and slapped his hand on his knee. "Ha. Like this doesn't happen around here?"

41

Diane sensed his disappointment. He'd told her earlier that dozens upon dozens of tips had come through in the first couple of weeks. He and Pete had sifted through everything from reports of loiterers, people parking funny, to a guy stuffing women's clothing into a vintage mailbox no longer in use.

"Yes, sir, it does happen," Sam agreed about the situation. "Sometimes tourists and drunks forget their manners."

Diane moved up to the edge of her chair. "And then what?"

"And...I'm getting ahead of myself," Sam said. "See, after I got to work that morning, a call came in for me to look at some property over on Cliff Road. I put my coat back on, took another phone call, and then I left. I came back down this direction and wanted to take an alley shortcut. But when I got there, I saw this guy and went around the end of the block instead, which took me longer. It didn't add up, really. He didn't look like a bum, but I figured he must've been from out of town because he didn't know where the public restrooms are."

Diane leveled her gaze on him. "Where was this?"

"What alley?" prompted McGuire further for the specific.

"That skinny one that runs along the east side of the Falcon Building." He sat up straighter, like he was about ready to leave. "He was leaking right next to the dumpster. There's only one of them along in there." He rolled his eyes. "That dumpster smells to high heaven in summer. You'd think the city would do somethin' about it. Anyway, I didn't think anything of it at the time. But then all this trouble came out about Arabella's murder, and with the TV announcements and all, it came back to me when I woke up this morning."

McGuire rolled his fingers on the table. "What *time* did you see the *offender*?"

Sam squared his shoulders. "No need to get prickly, guys. We have a guest present." He leaned toward Pete and whispered, "*Who* is she, anyway?"

Diane waved. "Diane Phipps, P.I. Please do go on."

Sam shrugged. "Well, by then, it had to be close to ten forty-five or eleven."

Diane stiffened. Instinct set in, but believing a tip coming from the guy who had the best motive to murder Arabella...rejection...

seemed a stretch. Ironic, really. Still, he'd stepped up to the plate to help, and what he was reporting seemed plausible.

"What'd he look like?" McGuire stopped rolling his fingers.

"Like any of the rest of us, the ones who don't live from bar to bar for their next drink, that is. Cowboy hat and dark jeans, I think. Boots." He lifted his hands. "I don't remember details too well, except his hat had fallen off. I barely caught him reaching up to get it with his free hand, while he was...you know."

Intrigued, Diane almost stood up to pace. "Reached up where?"

"Well, I could be wrong, but probably from the bottom of the fire escape behind him."

A pall dropped over the group.

Then, Roger McGuire suddenly laughed. "This is all rot. What guy do you know that takes off his hat to take a damned—"

"To relieve himself," Diane said. "Sam, how do you think it got up there?"

Sam circled his hand in the air, searching for sense. "Not sure. Fell off from when he jumped down to the ground? But it's like six feet down. Hell, I don't know, ma'am."

Again, the group fell silent as Sam pushed back his chair. "That's all I got, except that he seemed in a hurry. He grumbled down at his... self, 'C'mon, already.'" Sam pulled his jacket together. "I have to go. A new client's waiting. Like I said, might not be worth a hill of beans, but it's what I saw."

Detective McGuire nodded. "Good enough. Thank you." He then pointed at Pete. "Let's call Forensics back over to that alley."

"I'm on it. Snow's coming late tonight."

"Crap."

Sitting closest to the door, Diane led the way out of the room. Her senses from the scenario had stirred her mind into a bounty of questions. There were so many things to pin down yet in order to form solid conclusions. But one thing she knew for sure—tomorrow was another day. Also, information came from all kinds of sources. So, she would widen her net to catch more clues, starting at the Manitou Springs Library.

Seven

About the Dumbwaiter

Diane answered the door next morning and a cold gust of wind rushed in while she greeted Maria from next door. Snow was falling like mad as she looked over her neighbor's shoulder at her dark blue rental car parked by the curb. White mounds covered three-quarters of the wheels and the roof looked like a giant puffy marshmallow.

"Hi. I figured you weren't going to be out much today," Maria began. "They don't plow up here on Columbine Path, just so you know. This one's a wet one. But we're used to it."

Diane shivered. "You're a hardy bunch, that's for sure. Come on in, please."

Maria's snow-capped hair made her look like a snow queen wearing a white ermine hood. Her eyes were bright and smile was genuine. She was about five foot four and wore Nordic boots with faux fur running up the front. Her black quilted knee-length coat gave a serious semaphore for ugly weather.

While Maria stepped onto the flagstone entryway, Diane's thoughts raced to the forensic team trying to find and scrape urine samples from the ground in the alley—if they could even find the evidence. Three months of mountain weather had diminished that chance of gaining a DNA substance. Having one would help prove the killer's presence in the area. Trying to collect one now, so long after the fact, could be considered grasping for straws. But stranger things have happened to provide crucial evidence. There'd still be the issue of timing. Except Sam was a witness, which could nail it down considerably.

Maria shed her coat, and Diane hung it on a deer horn coat rack on the wall by the door. "Is the library open on days like this?" she asked. What looked to her like a blizzard waged war outside, but it was beautiful and breathtaking. Overall, it was sort of a shock to her system from having lived by the open sea and ever-changing clouds for the past years.

"We're supposed to have eleven inches. No big deal," Maria assured her. "Do you have boots?"

Diane shook her head to the negative. "Last time I saw snow like this was in St. Louis."

Interested, Maria asked, "Really? We've visited, seen the Cardinals play a game and gone to the art museum in Forest Park." She slowed for a moment. "That's when I still had my David..."

Diane pulled her flamingo-colored robe around herself. "I'm sorry for your loss. Would you like some coffee? I just made some, and yesterday I picked up some apple turnovers from Frankie's Bakery."

"Don't mind if I do," Maria chimed. "Then I'll call my friend Cherie. Her husband, Fred, has a four-wheeler, and he'll get us to the library. That is if you don't mind some company? Opens at ten on weekdays."

Diane looked at the stove clock showing 9:10. She wasn't up for company while focusing on news articles, but Maria was offering her a way to make use out of this day.

"Sure, I'll be looking at newspapers...for the case." She hoped Maria would catch the hint to give her some space and time alone.

Maria followed her into the kitchen. "Well, I'll be checking out the books on miniatures and the new DVDs. Florine's on duty today. We go back a way together. She was pretty torn up about what happened. Her niece, Debby, works at Frankie's. Everyone there was beside themselves when they found out a murder was going on upstairs over their heads." She sighed heavily. "The shop closed out of respect for the deceased. Arabella Laurens was a steady customer. Debby was the one who found the poor woman's scarf in their dumbwaiter two days later."

Diane widened her eyes. It had turned up days after the forensics sweep. She resigned herself to read more of Detective McGuire's reports.

"Do you take cream or sugar?" Diane asked as she poured the coffee.

"Cream, please. It was bizarre," Maria added. "The art woman had often ordered baked goods to have while she worked upstairs. She put in long hours. Debby began sending her orders up to her using the dumbwaiter back in the storage area. It's a rickety thing, but it worked and was convenient. The woman upstairs would pick up her fresh-out-of-the-oven cinnamon rolls or whatever and send the money back down to Debby in the paper sack. Well, after the bakery re-opened, Debby remembered that her then-deceased customer upstairs probably had sent her payment for the cinnamon roll she'd ordered for that awful morning. So, Debby went back and opened the dumbwaiter, and sure enough, there was the white sack."

"Well, that's a cool little system," Diane said, taking her first sip of coffee.

Maria's eyes misted. "They'd done that for a while, except this time there was a silk scarf wrapped around the neck of the bag in a droopy bow. Cherie said Debby got excited about it because it was a fine silk scarf. She figured the brownish stain marring the silk was just paint, and that the scarf was a gift from her customer, the art restorer." She stopped cold. "Well...that certainly turned out to not be the case."

Maria's hand shook and the cup jiggled. "Debby's dating Garth, one of our patrolmen. He was there when she found it, and he took it in as evidence. Luckily, she hadn't touched it."

Diane reached to steady the cup. "Thank you for telling me, and it is disturbing, for sure."

"Lord, I'd say. The whole thing had set this town on its ear." She visibly shuddered. "I'm double locking doors at night, and getting in before dark. It helps to know someone is in this place next door to me, too."

Diane fell quiet. *Fear.* This was what good people reaped for rotten people's crimes. Familiar disgust swirled up in her like a dust storm. It needed to be let out, which sharpened her goal to solve this case.

"I'll be keeping this conversation in mind," she said. "I can be ready for the library in twenty minutes."

She and Maria stood together. "Works for me, but it'll take Fred a while to get here. He lives over that way, higher up," she gave a quick point with her thumb. "Do you have boots, or not?"

Diane shook her head to the negative. She'd grandiosely given up her flip flops for this trip right into winter. As far as leaving comfortable foot gear behind, her effort was puny. But help was clearly on the way.

"Just my walking shoes," she answered. "Which have come in handy around here."

Maria grinned. "Layer up, girl, and I'll loan you my David's galoshes. He wasn't that big of a guy...except in his heart. Anyway, they're rubber and fit over your shoes with little black latches up the front."

Diane squinted, but thanked her. She only hoped she could move with all the stuff she needed to pile on just to be warm.

"We're off for an adventure," Maria said. "Now, Fred drives pretty fast...more than once he's gotten a ticket. But this snow ought to slow him down."

Diane closed the front door behind her. An adventure, indeed. She'd fallen into fresh info about how the murder weapon was obtained, and she hadn't even hit the library yet. She headed back to the little bedroom and pictured the pastry bag dressed up with the victim's scarf like a present. She lamented aloud, "What a sick way to ditch a murder weapon."

Another visit to police records was on her schedule. After all, it was a good day for reading and indoor chats.

Eight

Snowy Day at the Library

Forty-five minutes later, Diane riffled through a stack of dated *Pikes Peak Bulletins*, the weekly newspaper. She sat at a corner table by a window. It was a cozy nook where she could also watch the snow. Many stories covered the homicide. "Local Woman Found Dead," "City Mourns," and "Murder Unsolved," were some of the headlines that ran in larger than normal print.

All of the stories commended the victim's work and reputation. Some included quotes from those who knew her. "I will miss her," said Sophie Wilson, owner of Manitou Kitchen Shoppe. "Arabella was taking up cooking, and we had great chats about utensils and recipes."

"She had beautiful hair. I always looked forward to working on it for her," reported Amy Stieg, her hairdresser at Amy's Salon.

"Only person I'd ever trust with fixing up paintings," Richard Green, a local art critic, commented.

It was obvious to Diane that Arabella was well-plugged into the community. Her obituary mentioned her surviving family, no children, her studio work, her church, her education, and her interest in local concerts. Diane read any article she could find and came up with nothing new. She wasn't even sure what she was looking for. Anything that could lead to *something* substantial.

Maria came over to the table with an armload of DVDs. "Well, now I've got something to keep me company in this storm," she said. "And I found this new book on making miniatures for doll houses."

Diane smiled up at her. "You're doing better than me, then. I'll be ready in another ten minutes."

Maria nodded. "I'll be over there by the door. Fred texted. He's coming down the hill."

Diane closed her notebook and began restacking the papers into the neat pile she'd been given by Florine, the library clerk. A sadness came over her. Every article showed respect for Arabella Laurens. This, frankly, made Diane's job more difficult. She had no answers, no primary suspect, no motive yet. She'd just have to keep on trucking, as her dad would've said. About to rise from the chair, she slowed as another patron walked up to her.

He was about six feet tall, with grey hair pulled back into a tail, and wearing an olive-green parka.

"Hi, don't mean to interrupt you, but have you been here very long? I'm to meet someone here at this table and am running a bit late. She was scheduled to offer a talk here today. Her name is Arabella."

Diane gazed at him with interest. "Not long, no. But..." she said softly. *Should I say, or not?* Being the bearer of bad news never thrilled her. She didn't know this gentleman, but he definitely had an attachment to the victim. He could come undone at the news. Books could be flying. At least there weren't many people in the library this morning. Florine had even said they'd probably close early.

The man locked his gaze on her and waited.

She girded herself. "Sir, the lady has passed away."

Taken aback, the man pulled out a chair and sank down. He laid the bundle he was carrying in front of him and worried the corners with his leather-gloved fingers.

"Oh my, this is terrible."

"Yes, it is," Diane agreed. "A lot of people think so, too."

He seemed at a loss, and cleared his throat. "My name's Angelo Barnes. Ms. Laurens and I had set this appoint the last time I came through town. It's about art, you see." He patted the soft case in front of him. "She was going to do some work for my client."

Diane lowered her chin. "I'm sorry."

Angelo still looked aghast. "How'd this happen?"

"Mr. Barnes, she was...murdered."

"What!" He glanced at the papers in front of her. "I hadn't heard. Good Lord!"

Sadness crossed his weathered face. He was a large built man with a goatee and expressive eyes.

"My name's Diane Phipps. I'm helping the local police find out who did it."

He peered at her and almost whispered, "Someone's going to be really upset about this."

Diane leaned closer. "I'll do my best."

"No, I mean about Arabella dying." He shook his head with remorse. "I don't know how I'm going to tell her..." His voice trailed off.

Instinct rumbled around in Diane. "Who's going to be so upset?" she pressed gently.

Angelo shook his head from side to side. "It's confidential. I'm sorry."

Diane couldn't let it go and she handed him a card from her bag. "Mr. Barnes, I'm doing everything I can to get to the bottom of this case. If you can help with any bit of information, you'll be the man of the hour, and I could sure use a fresh lead about now. I've been through this whole stack of papers and much more, and nothing's pointing to anything unusual. People know things about victims. And, it seems to me, you're busting at the gills with something here. So, if you can find it in yourself to share it with me, you'll be gaining angel wings...and a coffee on me."

Angelo leaned back. He obviously hadn't been ready for any of this when he had walked in. The battle going on in him swept over his face. He looked out at the snow and back at her.

"I suppose it doesn't matter now," he said gravely, more to himself than her.

Diane waited another moment. Timing was everything sometimes. When to push and when not, when people opened up about deep things. She sensed what Angelo had to share was as deep and dark as the Mariana Trench.

He snared her gaze as she repeated, "*Who's* going to be so upset, please?"

Angelo exhaled with a rush. "Her daughter."

Diane jolted further back into the chair. "Her *daughter?*"

"Yes, ma'am. She's eighteen, safe, and lives in Milan with a good family who owns a cosmetic firm. They adopted her. I'm her courier. The beginnings of her personal collection are in here. Small, but rare and fine paintings." He tapped the case. "Arabella was to clean them."

Diane's mind raced. "Wait. How does Arabella have a daughter?"

"She'd studied in Milan years ago. Met the guy there...they were young, and so it went."

Stymied, Diane asked, "Are you sure?"

He opened his billfold and showed her a picture.

Diane looked at every detail she could. A definite resemblance to the photos she'd seen of Arabella Laurens with her upturned nose, dark eyes and hair, and heart-shaped facial structure.

"Well, *this* is extraordinary. Thank you."

"It's also time for me to go. No time for coffee. Please don't make a fuss."

Diane nodded. "May I have her name, please?"

"It's Francesca. That's all. Francesca. Good luck, madam."

With that, Angelo plucked the bag up from the table and made a beeline out of the library.

Diane pulled her wits together and got up. Hoping to spot him, she scooted to the front door where Maria was waiting.

"Did you see a man just leaving here?" she asked in a rush.

Maria looked up from the book she was holding. Diane's intense expression must have alerted her. Wide-eyed she asked, "What man? No, I didn't. Hey, are you okay?"

Diane stopped in her tracks. "Sure, I just...Well, never mind."

Maria turned to look out the door. "Oh, look. Fred just pulled up. Let's go, okay?"

Diane returned to the cozy nook table, picked up her things, slipped into her coat, and headed outdoors to meet Fred. Her borrowed floppy galoshes squeaked against the floor with every step she took. "Drop me off at the P.D.?"

Nine

Blue, Not Black

Wayward elk, four of them, crossing Manitou Avenue delayed Diane's arrival at Detective McGuire's office. He actually smiled when he saw her. "What brings you out on this lovely day?"

"I just saw elk!" Diane first exclaimed. "They're huge, a*nd* I have news."

She laid most of it out. McGuire scratched his eyebrow and repeated, "Arabella Laurens has a daughter?"

"Apparently."

"That's juicy," he said. "Who's the father?"

She shrugged. "And, where is he?"

Diane dropped into her own thinking, and it looked like McGuire followed suit. Her mind played leap frog over implications. This new tip threw a handful of possible motives into the mix. Was there a dad who didn't want anyone to know? Then, again, did the father even know he had a daughter? Or even, what difference had it made that Arabella had offspring? Maybe none.

Offspring. Another motive possibility sprouted for Diane. *Did Arabella have insurance? Did she leave a will?* Maybe somebody didn't like the beneficiary list? Seemed a long shot, but she grew curious about Arabella's brother, Leo. If there was a will, was he included as a beneficiary?

Detective McGuire's voice interrupted. "We found insurance papers, tax records, bills, mementos like menus and pamphlets at her place. And vinyl records. She had a turntable. Don't see that much anymore. The rest was usual stuff. All that was turned over to her parents. We've not inquired further about beneficiaries." He took a labored breath. "An obvious oversight."

Diane raised an eyebrow and thought ahead aloud. "Her brother Leo is coming here next week to clear the storage space where he'd put more of her things until he could get back down to pick up the rest. I'm looking forward to meeting him...and his girlfriend, Willow Stonehaven."

She sat in the chair by his desk. The radio was on, country music coming at her from Nash 95.1. Made her feel all homey.

"What was Arabella's apartment like?"

"Not that fancy, but artsy. She lived in a four-plex over on Pinon Terrace. It's been re-rented."

Diane wasn't surprised. Addresses here probably went like hot cakes.

"She was a clothes nut," Detective McGuire remarked. "She must've had fifty scarves."

Diane smiled. She could relate. At one time, she couldn't get enough shoes. But Tom helped her straighten that out. Now it was sea shells. She rarely came home from a beach walk, after the tide had gone out, without a new one.

"What's the daughter's name?" McGuire asked.

"Francesca. That's all Barnes would give me. She's eighteen, lives in Milan."

McGuire was letting that sink in.

"Do you think there's a nervous dad involved here?" Diane probed.

Knitting his bushy brows together, the detective mindlessly tapped a forefinger on the desk. "Hard to say. If so, he's been nervous for eighteen years."

"Feelings build up," she said. "Then again, the dad might not know he has a daughter."

"Or, the cash could've been hush money," he threw out.

Diane nodded. That seemed believable, but it didn't hit her intuitive Ah ha! gong. "Maybe she wouldn't take it?"

McGuire pursed his lips. "Trouble in the Land of Secrets." His dry wit escaped again. It lightened the moment.

"I wonder how much cash there was."

"Enough to keep the lady quiet. Probably thousands is my guess."

"Monthly?"

McGuire pointed a you-got-it finger at her. "She wasn't a cheap date."

Diane grinned. "Babies cost a lot of money."

"So can reputations." But whose?

Still not totally buying the theory, Diane shook her head. "I don't know...something's not right, something went wrong."

"For her it did, anyway."

He handed Diane another folder, a thick one, tucked into a large plastic evidence bag. "Here's some more reading material for you."

She accepted it eagerly. Apparently, computers weren't the total answer. The staff here still copied key reports to paper for major cases and portability.

"We'll run Angelo Barnes through the system," he said. "What'd he look like?" She gave him a description to be admired. "Never underestimate your gum shoe eye for detail and impressions," Tom had once said. McGuire went on, "We'll see what we come up with. You should get back home. They've changed the forecast. We're looking at fourteen inches by tonight."

Diane blinked. "It sure knows how to snow around here."

"It's a good year," he grunted. "More snow, more water. A good thing, unless it floods again like hell."

"I'm hoping for a ride," she said, pulling on her mittens.

McGuire obliged and turned to a patrolman. "Sergeant Marty, give the lady a ride home."

The going was slow, fifteen miles an hour in a fully-equipped squad SUV. They rode by the Falcon Building, the post office, and assorted shops. She planned to drop in on some of them while she was there. One with wooden carved bears had caught her eye. Many had their lights on, but a lot of parking places were empty. Pikes Peak was lost in the snow.

Twenty-eight degrees showed on her cell phone. There was little breeze, and the flakes fell straight down. It seemed like a winter wonderland to her. Tree branches sagged, and the mailbox posts were disappearing. Was it snowing in Montana? she wondered.

Once they were back at her temporary place on Columbine Path, the sergeant had to help her push open the front gate, and the brick pavement had vanished. She plodded forward, holding the plastic bag close to her heart, and used the small front porch as a destination reference.

It'd been quite a day so far. All she could think about now was hot chocolate...and getting in the front door without falling face forward from the funky galoshes that were too big.

~ * ~

Diane couldn't believe how quiet it was the next morning. She sat in the kitchen having coffee and checked out the back yard. Moose printed curtains framed the window. Such a change from pink hibiscus, she thought. Outside the windows, one pine tree seemed to blend into the next one, and so on.

She shifted her attention back to the file folders she'd opened the night before and left on the table. The pink bill of lading from the couriers who delivered the art work to Arabella lay on top of one pile. Each man had initialed it, and Arabella's signature of receipt was large and curly.

It tugged at her heart looking at something as personal as the deceased's signature. Nothing was so haunting as fingerprints left behind, signatures, or clothes in the dirty laundry pile. Which made her think about how Arabella had collected scarves. From the photos Diane had seen, the one she wore on the day she died was extraordinary. It was high style and probably high dollar. She'd tried to see the label, but wasn't able. From where had it come?

The bill of lading was printed in large block letters. Easy to read on the copy which she surmised was provided to Arabella before they left. The couriers' initials were scribbled in haste, one under the other. CJH. ATP. Setting it aside, she almost missed another set in the lower right-hand corner. They were barely legible. Undoubtedly, a set-up release by a supervisor back at the office.

Her cell phone rang. It was on the charger in the living room. She pushed herself to her slippered feet and picked it up off the solid wood coffee table. McGuire's voice came through when she answered.

"Are you faring okay up there?" he asked.

"A bit chilly." She glanced at the fireplace. "I'm not a good fire builder."

McGuire chuckled. "We won't hold that against you."

But it was true. It was another reason she wished for Tom to be with her. She longed to hear from him again. She'd learned long ago that calling him wasn't a good idea. Her calls went nowhere while he was on classified duty. She missed her house, too. The only other thing that'd make her feel closer to home would be seeing a seagull. But there wasn't one to be found.

The detective's tone turned serious. "I'm calling with something to add to your notes. The denim fiber found under the victim's nails is black. And here's something else from Forensics. A hair was found, short and gray, and they're still working on that."

Diane perked up. *Evidence.* It made all the difference in the world. She quickly jotted down the new notes and dated them. Little by little, they were propelling her toward truth.

Arabella Lauren had been wearing indigo blue jeans that day, not black...

Ten

Family Matters

Snow kept things slow for the next day, although it was starting to melt. Diane used the indoor time to sift through notes and work on her portable crime case board. She'd written Arabella's name in a circle in the center and drawn lines from it to the growing list of names of people in her life and those who popped up with information. It all formed a big circle, kind of like a flower with petals, with Arabella being in the center. The schematic helped for a quick at-a-glance view.

She'd had lunch before someone knocked at the front door. Quickly, she smoothed her hair, straightened her long-sleeve shirt, and adjusted the front of her sweater. The thought that she'd be in shorts, a tank top, and flip flops back home gave her the shivers as she opened the door and the cold air smacked her.

"Hi," the gentleman greeted. He looked like Santa, sort of, with a white beard and his longish hair escaping from beneath a cap with ear flaps. "I'm Eugene Ketchum. I'm a friend of Maria's next door. She told me you were here. Wanted to see you for a minute, if you have time? The Falcon Building is my property."

Diane slowly smiled, stretched out her hand for a shake. As far as she was concerned, she suddenly had all the time in the world. "Please, come in," she said, and in another two minutes he sat at her kitchen table with some hot coffee in front of him.

The weather came up as the first topic, then Eugene said, "I have Ms. Lauren's studio rent check for January." He pulled out an envelope from a pocket of his outdoor vest. "I'm not keeping it. Wondering if you could see that her family gets it?"

Diane eyed the envelope. The flourish of the handwriting on it resembled Arabella's signature on the bill of lading. "I can do that for you, yes. Leo Lauren will be here soon, and I'll pass it on to him."

Eugene hesitated handing it to her. "That might not be a good idea. Granted, he's listed as her emergency contact on her lease application, but I'm not so sure it should go to him."

Diane raised her chin. His reaction seemed a shock. She leaned forward. "He's very upset she's gone, you know. How come you feel this way?"

The building owner scratched his head. "About a week before she died, I'd gone up to the studio to meet her to make a list of things that needed done. When I got off the elevator, I heard shouting. Loud shouting. I recognized her voice, and she was hot into an argument with Leo. So, I'm not so sure they got along. And if they didn't, he might not be of mind to pass this along to her parents."

Diane's interest sizzled. "How do you know it was Leo? Had you met him before?"

"Can't say that I had," he said. "But she repeated his name twice. 'Leo, none of this is your business. Leave us alone, Leo,' she'd yelled. Then he hollered back, 'It's *our* family.'"

"Well, this wasn't a good time for making a repair list, so I left," Eugene explained.

Leo and Arabella really didn't get along? Or was this a short spat between siblings?

"What do you think they were talking, or yelling about?" Diane asked.

"I'm thinking it had to do with James, her new boyfriend."

"Did she say his name during this?"

Eugene nodded. "Just as I hit the elevator, she cried, 'I'll marry who I want. And James is him!' Long about then, one or the other of them was opening the studio door to walk out. I figured it was Leo, but I'd jumped the gun on him with the elevator and got to ground level first. I left the building and turned to look back when I got a few doors up. He was leaving the side door in a huff. Have you met him?"

"Not yet," Diane told him. "But I'll keep this in mind when I do. Anyway, I understand your concern. Detective McGuire will have her parents' address. Maybe you should return the check to them?"

Eugene's expression saddened. "I've lost a good tenant with her. She was never late on her rent. She treated the place as if it was hers. She'd earned her full deposit back. I'll be sending that on to her parents, too."

Diane sipped more coffee. "Fair of you."

"No problem. If something went wrong with the place, she reported it to me. Not complaining, either. She'd asked nicely. I agreed to keep the place off the available list for ninety days for the police work. But that's almost over. So, my connection to her will soon be total history."

He stopped long enough for another sip. "Tell you what, though. James Boyd is a solid, good guy. Ms. Laurens had good taste."

Diane could understand his sentiment. Yet, when she had met James, there was no mention of a strained meeting between him and Leo. Quite the opposite. But difficulties can get resolved within families and not everyone knows. Thus, Eugene's report might be dated. Except, this kind of hot blowup seemed to be deep-seated and serious. Not the type of issue to be resolved overnight.

What Eugene said he heard had happened merely days before Arabella was found dead. So wouldn't it be likely that Leo's contempt was still cooking by the time of Arabella's funeral when James had met him face to face? Diane tucked this tidbit away in her mind to watch for covert friction during her time with them. More strangely, why would Leo be so angry about James? Time and perhaps a few subtle questions would tell. Probing into family matters wasn't her style...but, this was about murder.

~ * ~

A day later, Diane pulled on and latched up poor old David's galoshes and tromped out the front door. The snow had melted quite a bit. Yesterday she'd figured it'd take a week to make her way to her rental car. But the overall low humidity—so different from Florida—was doing its evaporative magic. So much so, she'd driven down to Adam's Mountain Cafe with no mishap and parked to meet Pam, who called her for lunch.

Investigations often took her to many doors and people. Sometimes, friendships ignited. It had happened with Kitty Swan, her neighbor in Atlantic Beach, who'd lost her granddaughter Chelsea, aka Mermaid Nerissa. During investigations, it was good to be around folks who knew victims well. Little things came up that seemed insignificant at the time, yet had bearing on cases at hand. Diane just needed to know what to listen for.

Pam wore a rust-colored turtle neck sweater and denim blue jeans, the fabric and style of choice of the American West. Black jeans were favored, too, along with black hats with silver trims. She was seeing lots of silver and turquoise in shop windows. But Pam wore strands of polished amber, which complemented her auburn hair.

"Thanks for asking me for lunch," Diane began and made choices from the menu.

"Ara and I used to come here," Pam said. "We usually sat over there." She pointed to a table nearby.

Diane nodded and asked, "How're you doing?"

"I don't have any sisters. She was my closest friend, so it's been difficult. Any closer to finding the killer?"

Diane wished for more than, "Some things have come up." She drank some water with no ice. Things were cold enough here. "How'd you get into the jewelry business?"

Pam smiled. "I've always loved gemstones, rocks, and precious stones, too. But geology wasn't my thing. Tried creating copper wire neck pieces and bracelets for a while, but it wasn't hitting my creative mark. I wanted more from the medium. I wanted color, glimmer, shine and shapes." She gave her order to the server. "Then, learning the meanings of gems added another element," she added, "People are drawn to certain ones. That all took me deeper into designing unique wearable art. I do okay with it. People like my stuff."

Diane admired her. "I can see why. What you're wearing is lovely." She definitely seemed at peace with it all.

"I'd made pieces for Ara," she said. "She liked lapis lazuli. Blue, her favorite color, you know. Then, she was drawn to moonstones. I thought it was curious. But people have moods or things happen that affect them, and they find beauty in something different for a while. I found some exceptional moonstones and made her a triple tier necklace. I was afraid I'd gone overboard with it, but it turned out to be her favorite."

"Was moonstone her birthstone?"

"Emeralds."

Diane agreed. A curious point. "I wonder why moonstones? What's their meaning?"

"First, they're in the Feldspar family. Have an amazing iridescent quality, like looking at moonlight. Popular Art Nouveau stone, and they resurged again during the Flower Child era. Seem to have spirit moving in them. A stone for visionaries. Gives off a subtle blue flash. Its sense of secrecy and mystery appeals to some."

Diane leaned forward. "Did Arabella have deep secrets, do you think?"

Pam raised her chin. "You'd wondered about that before."

"I'm wondering again, sorry. Have you ever sensed something at work in her she was unwilling to share?"

Pam looked at her dead on. "If it's important to her case, the answer is...yes, I have caught glimpses, you know?"

Diane asked, "Any hints what she was keeping quiet?"

"Something sad," she said quickly. "I think she threw herself into her work more than the rest of us, if that counts for anything. She studied hard and long for her career. She once mentioned that her art restoration program was for two years, but she'd spent an extra year in Italy."

Diane chewed her salad thoughtfully. "She must've made friends while she was there."

"She made friends everywhere. James was crazy about her."

"D'you think he'd have married her?"

"Three times over," she said smiling.

The scenario gave Diane a warm rush. "They'd have stayed here?"

Pam lifted her fork. "Sure."

"Planned to have family?"

Pam shook her head from side to side. "That'd be a no. Ara's biological clock was ticking, but she wasn't in a rush to have children. James didn't seem to mind, either." She paused. "Some couples are like that. They have each other, and that's enough."

Diane was tempted to mention Mr. Barnes and his news. But her professional discretion won out. Also, it brought to mind that her own biological clock was ticking. Having had two miscarriages, she and Tom had pretty much decided not to be parents. So, she understood "enough."

Their work kept them from having a dog, too. After she and Tom had relocated to NE Florida and Tom began being away for stretches of time, she thought it a good idea to have a cat. But even that could be a challenge. Luckily, Kitty back home watered the potted hibiscus and indoor plants for her while she was away, for which she was grateful. She did like growing things...and lately collecting shells.

Pam ordered another iced tea and dug into her salad. She seemed more relaxed today, more open to chatting and reminiscing. "Ara liked fashion accessories. She could put a scarf on with faded jeans and a sweat shirt and look sharp."

"I heard about her scarf collection," Diane offered.

Pam grinned. "It was *quite* the thing. James put up little pegs in her closet to hold them. She had favorite scarves, too. Several were gifts to her. From worldwide markets, I think."

Diane summoned up the image of the murder weapon—an interesting scarf with a narrow hand rolled and stitched black and gold border. Iridescent butterflies were strewn across the silk. Lots of color. For sure, Arabella Laurens didn't shy away from wearing color.

"She had a few I really liked, too," Pam fluttered her hands while she spoke. "One had butterflies all over it. A Liz Ricci."

Diane sucked in a breath instead of closing her eyes. Her thoughts leaped ahead. She doubted that specific scarf, which ended up being a murder weapon, would ever be made public, except at trial. Crossing her fingers that Pam wouldn't be present for that, she slipped in, "Probably her family has it." It seemed the kind thing to say. She wasn't about to crush this woman's warm memories.

"I wonder where she got it?" Diane asked lightly.

Pam shrugged. "Maybe from a friend from long ago while she was in the study program? Going back to Milan and Florence was on her wish list. But...it'll never happen."

Diane sprung an idea. "Maybe someday you should go for Arabella. See the jewelry, fashion, and sights. Keep her in your steps along the way."

Pam teared up. "I try to do that now."

Hours later, Diane made more notes and drew an empty circle on the white board. She drew its connector line right to the middle of Arabella's name. Just where a mom would keep her child—unwanted or otherwise—in her heart.

Eleven

Timing?

The next day Diane checked in with Detectives McGuire and Woodrow. They ran a fast recount of what they knew and what they didn't know. Despite the rehash, more questions than answers were still coming up. Hopefully, one end of that seesaw would soon hit ground. She hoped for a resounding thud when it did.

They chewed over the newest clue. "The dude was wearing black jeans," McGuire said, looking up from a new report. "Sam Crawford reported the guy in the alley was in dark clothes."

"And a hat," Woodrow slipped in.

"We're lucky Sam was in the right place at the right time to see him," Diane said.

McGuire got up and refilled his coffee mug. "We need a helluva lot more than that."

"Right on," Pete said and slapped Roger's desk.

"Timing is everything," McGuire called back somewhat sarcastically to them from over his shoulder.

Diane looked at their cluttered gray board and went to it. She picked up a marker from the tray, and squeezed in TIMING on the surface. No other notes had been made about that aspect. All of which got her thinking.

"So, two things come up for me," she began as McGuire sat back down behind his desk. He gave her the nod to go on. "The first is: *Why* was Arabella Laurens murdered *when* she was?"

Pete gave her a thumbs-up for it.

"How come it happened then?" she struggled on. "Working on the Monet would probably have taken her weeks, giving the killer plenty of time to make his move. So, why'd he pick that day and time, that moment?" She lifted her hands in question. "Why did he look at it as a window of opportunity?"

Detectives McGuire and Woodrow exchanged glances.

"Good point," McGuire put in.

"That question needs an answer," Pete Woodrow said.

"Might help us figure this whole thing out," Diane suggested. Between this and a viable motive, her thoughts rumbled in her head. But motive still stood queen, reigning over secrecy. Walter Haverstone thought it happened because of attempted theft. It was his most valuable possession besides Stonegate, so it stood to reason he'd feel most vulnerable about those things, thus putting it on the map as a motive. She couldn't get past that, either.

Pete asked point blank. "What's the second thing?"

"Jumping track, a bit, from timing to motive," she began, "Was Arabella's murder for the sake of getting rid of her? Or, did her death occur because of a botched theft?"

Woodrow sneezed and reached for a Kleenex. "Either way, she's dead," he said from behind the tissue. "We still need a suspect."

He'd just lost the Best Diplomacy Award, but Diane concurred. "If he went in to steal the painting, something unexpected happened. He left empty-handed."

"Right," McGuire said. "The Monet was left behind at the scene."

Diane shook her head. "What a bad turn...for the painting, I mean. Some of the surface got spotted with paint."

"Black oil paint," Pete put in bluntly.

"Black?" Diane inquired. She'd remembered seeing the dark stain on the green felt.

McGuire confirmed. "Came through from Forensics; it's an update."

"How destructive," Diane said, noting it in her little book. "The best person to clean it off is no longer here," slipped out from her as an aside.

All three took a breather. They'd been at it for an hour already.

Woodrow leaned back in his chair, stretched and crooked his arms behind his head. His ruffled hair looked as if it hadn't been combed this morning. A bit of stubble covered his jaw and chin. Lots of women would consider him a hunk, Diane figured. Which showed her head needed a break. Elements of this case had taken up permanent residency in her mind. Day and night, separate pieces of info and clues ran around looking for partners and what made the most sense.

"Let's focus on theft first," she said, hoping the process of elimination would do the trick. "Who knew the Monet was coming?"

McGuire stepped up to the plate. "The Haverstones, some of their staff, the courier company, James Boyd, and Pam Piper. Maybe others?"

Diane had believed so, but asked anyway. She was still catching up with details that were established before she arrived.

"All trusted people," she noted aloud.

"With documented movement, too," McGuire added.

"How'd it go with interviewing the couriers?" she asked.

"Two guys. They came out...not carrying anything," Pete said.

"As it should've been if they left the painting for her to work on," McGuire said.

"How'd we find that out?" she asked.

"Adam Perinsky, the guy from the fly shop next door, was taking out his trash and saw them leaving her studio. They were wearing jumpsuits," McGuire said. "Clean backgrounds, both of the men. Bonded."

"So, *who* was the guy Sam saw in the other alley?" Diane asked.

"Maybe nobody," Pete Woodrow suggested. "No connection."

"Maybe everybody," Diane said resolutely. "Every connection." Her strong hunch told her he was the culprit. But identifying him and proving it was another whole challenge.

Diane's cell phone rang. She glanced at the screen. "Tom!" she exclaimed, and her heart warmed. She waved bye-bye at the detectives. "Excuse me, I need to take this call."

Exiting the building, she stopped out in the parking lot. "Hello, dear," he said, coming through loud and strong. "Meet me by the town clock in thirty?"

Diane choked up. "You're here?" Maybe this case was getting to her more than she thought. She needed fortifying, the kind she'd get from her husband.

"I'm on borrowed time, so don't be late," he said. "We have one hour."

"I'll take it," she said, eager for his hugs and to run some things by him.

~ * ~

So, there he was. Tom in all his glory, looking regular, but it was hardly so. Carrying a sandwich bag from a local shop and soda in a Thermos, Diane walked up to him.

"Fancy meeting you *here*, on a Friday morning," she joked.

He grinned. "Sorry it's so short. Dipped away from the team to do this. We're on a run south down the I-25 corridor." He pointed. "Is that lunch?"

Diane shook the bag. "Roast beef for you on a fresh hoagie bun."

Appreciation lit up his face. "Good. Have been eating crap on this assignment. Except for Twizzlers," he said and winked. "I passed a little park on the way here. Let's head there."

Settled at a picnic table against a tree, Diane and he shared soda from the same cup.

He then gave her a quick once-over. "You look wrought up."

She was. He opened the door to spilling whatever she could remember about the case. Tom was a good listener, and an even better observer. She mentioned the people involved, those whom she'd met and whom she'd hadn't. "I'll have a chance to meet the victim's brother this coming week. I have mixed feelings about him." She munched on some chips. "And I'm in the complete dark about a motive. And the crime. Was it murder, or a botched theft with murder attached? Different crimes, different motives."

Tom looked at his watch. She'd given it to him two years ago for Christmas. It had every outfitter accessory known to man built into it. She grasped at every minute ticking by. Her time with Tom was precious to her. Just being in his presence fed her energy.

When she wound down from talking, Tom reminded her, "Sounds like you've covered a lot of ground." He reached over and squeezed her hand. "Don't forget to put yourself in the perp's place."

She squeezed back. "Got it. Any idea when you'll be done?"

"Not yet. It's convoluted," he said in undertones. "Tracking some bad-assed gun runners."

She marveled over the kinds of classified situations Tom took on. Variety certainly existed in the world of crime.

He nodded at her boots. "Whose are they?"

"They're borrowed from David, a dead guy. Maria's late husband. She lives next door to the cottage rental. The place is cozy with big pine trees in the back. There's a fireplace I haven't lit yet."

He snorted, checking out the boot latches. "Those boots aren't doing you any favors, luv. Buy some you like."

"The thought has crossed my mind," she said.

"Then do something about it."

"Are they that bad?"

"Yes," he said emphatically.

Twenty minutes later, they hugged goodbye. He left her and headed east on foot. The weather was warming up a bit, so more folks were out. She watched him until he drifted into the crowd. For the rest of her day, Diane carried his advice in her head and heart, hearing his deep voice all the while. *Buy boots and put myself in the perp's place.*

Twelve

Her Brother

Diane linked up with James, as planned, to meet Leo Laurens and his girlfriend, Willow. Considering how Leo was supposed to be so at odds with James, James didn't seem at all nervous about them getting together again that afternoon. To Diane, that meant James wasn't at all aware of Leo's true opinion about James' plan to marry Leo's sister. So, she'd be testing the waters, as it were, to see if Leo popped loose with dismay at any time. Still, she wasn't out there to bring James any more bad news.

He drove her over to the storage shed in Colorado City, the next town down the road. They found Leo and Willow waiting by a rented U-Haul truck and greeted them warmly, with James introducing her. "She's been hard at work," he said, as she shook Leo's hand.

"This is good news. We appreciate you," Leo said, gazing at the shed. "We really need to get to the bottom of this." He turned and opened the storage door with a tug.

Willow stood next to Diane while the two guys went to work. Diane side-glanced her. She had long blonde hair and wore fashionable bracelets on her wrist. During their visit for the funeral, James had mentioned she was a quiet girl. Seemed unlikely she was shy, and they were all there for a somber reason.

If it were true about Leo and Arabella quarreling days before she died, the last person Diane had expected to start talking about her would be Leo. He probably felt guilty. Diane chose not to mention Arabella's name. But when Willow saw the guys carrying out one of Arabella's quilts, she stopped them. "Wait, please. That was the quilt my mother gave Arabella when she'd come up to visit with my dad about cleaning the painting. It was Arabella's birthday and she was still doing business. My mom thought that was very gracious of her."

Leo walked over to her and handed the rolled-up bundle to her. "Here, you keep this."

His eyes narrowed and his gaze darted over to James, who was loading a chair into the truck.

"This way it'll stay in the family."

"Thank you," Willow said and wrapped her arms around the cloth.

Diane smiled. It was a nice gesture, yet she heard the edge in Leo's tone. It nearly betrayed the friendliness shown to James when they'd arrived. So brief, hardly noticeable, but *there*. She stepped out of the way while the two men carried a folding table past her.

"How about we all go for a bite after this?" she suggested as they regathered.

"Sure. Would love it," Willow said. The guys followed suit.

An hour later found them back at Casey's Hut with mega burgers in front of them.

"I'd come down here again just for one of these," Willow said after the server brought everyone's orders. Obviously, stress brought on hunger.

Diane said lightly after taking a couple of bites, "I would, too."

James gave a laugh. "Kind of a long way to come for a burger."

Leo said, "You're here from Florida?"

"A flatlander checking in for duty," she quipped.

Smiling, Willow said, "Well, I for one am glad you're working on this case. Seems like it needs all the hands it can get. Everyone at home is still upset."

"Completely understandable," Diane said.

"Yesterday, Yves took down the empty frame he'd hung up," Willow offered. "A Maxfield Parrish is up there now in that space. At first, our curator was in denial about the Monet being out of reach. But he's coming around to accept it."

Leo nodded. "It was a terrible loss and situation."

James agreed. "I'm still wrung out. I'd picked out a ring for her."

A grave and solemn expression rode rampant over Leo's face.

Willow shook her head. "It's just so puzzling how or why this could've happened."

Diane sighed. "Amen to that." She'd found that cases seemed to have their own will. This one meandered and seemed full of mayhem at the moment. Still, she sensed she was getting closer to finding answers, albeit little chips at a time. Eventually, though, they led to big chunks of facts. Amen, again.

Willow added, "My father is very cautious about the art collection. Moving any of it is always a risk. The courier company was highly recommended. Even so, I'd walked into the stable one day, and he was talking with Rydell." She stopped and said for Diane's benefit, "He's the guy who takes care of our horses, shoes them, and walks the fences for security. Lusitanos are valuable, and someone might get the idea to steal one."

"I see," Diane said thoughtfully. "Classic case of taking what's not yours to build empires."

James put in, "Like certain cattle rustlers who helped develop this state."

Leo nodded at him in agreement.

"Anyway," Willow went on. "My dad and Rydell were talking about Rydell riding along during the transport of the Monet, just to make sure the couriers did their job with the delivery. Rydell thanked him for the trust, then told my dad flat out he'd rather not."

Leo said, "Probably so. Rydell kinda has a temper. Willow's mom Ruth told me one time she'd seen him cussing out a bear for ripping up a fence post. Barbed wire went flying. Wasn't pretty. He got a scar on his hand out of that."

Diane struggled to suppress a laugh. *Oh, the colorful West.*

Leo dribbled ketchup on his fries, and asked Diane, "So, are you making progress?"

His question drew everyone's attention. She lifted the quiet with, "I'm forming impressions, pulling facts together. Slowly, I admit. For now, I'm still in the hunting and gathering stage."

"Interesting," James said. His grey and brown plaid flannel shirt offset the interest flickering in his eyes. "What happens next?"

Diane hesitated. "When I know the whole picture, I'll make my move."

Normally, she wouldn't have revealed that, but this group was so connected to the victim she wanted to give them hope. Even so, she kept in mind that victims were often killed by people they knew. So, until she'd uncovered the truth, she trained a watchful eye on everyone and kept a keen ear to the ground. It was wearing, though, being a sleuth and a friend. Precarious, even.

~ * ~

Diane sifted through more police files at home. She'd opened her laptop and made a detailed list of every person mentioned for any reason, including those she'd met who weren't in the reports and those names other folks had mentioned who were part of Arabella's life. They were either primary contacts like close friends and immediate family, secondary contacts like folks in the neighborhood, or tertiary connections like the counterpersons at the grocery store. Her world was full and her career ambitions kept her on track.

Most likely, her membership in the Front Range Art Society had helped Arabella with her work. When James Boyd had told Diane a special gala of the organization was coming up in Colorado Springs and extended an invitation to her, she jumped at the chance to go—if she were still there.

She liked dress-up affairs and had brought one black dressy dress along in case she ran into the need for it. The gala was ten days away at 7:00 p.m. at the Hotel Eleganté, and she marked it on her calendar.

Meanwhile, Detective McGuire contacted her.

"Your friend Angelo Barnes isn't Angelo Barnes. We think it's an alias."

Diane removed a bowl of bison stew from the microwave. Maria had dropped it off the night before, but after she'd had her own dinner of canned soup and crackers.

"An alias for whom?"

"A guy named Bob Smith."

Diane rolled her eyes. "Well, good luck with that one. There must be thousands of Bob Smiths in the country."

McGuire grunted, "About forty-six thousand. We're getting help from Denver."

Diane shook her head. This case was getting more difficult as the days wore on. She saw nothing but a hodge-podge of people, loose connections, and starts with no finishes. Frustration took root in her.

Am I trying too hard? shot through her mind. It wasn't the first time she'd encountered this cornered feeling. Bits and pieces were falling on top of her, instead of her being on top of them. The crime board in the small bedroom was nearly filled with little notes and flower petal people.

Times like this made her throw her hands up and ask herself, "Whose idea was this, anyway?" about devoting her life to solving crimes. Tom wouldn't feel this way, she was sure. He used a "put one foot in front of the other, deduction, logic, and keep your eyes open" approach. It continually paid off for him.

Diane's inner voice whispered, "Patience."

Thirteen

Only Two Hands

Later that night, Diane slipped her feet into warm socks and slippers. Tom's reminder words *put yourself into the shoes of the culprit* rose in her thoughts about new boots. The snow had melted and the temperature in Manitou today was seventy-one. Maria said spring was teasing them. It did get down in the twenties where she and Tom lived in NE Florida. She just never followed up with buying boots, although a lot of women wore those popular Australian ones.

So, maybe now was the time, and she moved the idea up on her priority list. For some reason, she wondered if the killer had worn boots. What had gone wrong? hit her again. Thinking further, it occurred to her that if theft had been the plan, it was a poor one. There was one detail that required forethought that he'd missed. The Monet painting was large...and heavy. It had taken two men to deliver it up to Arabella's studio. So, how'd he think he was going to pull off carrying it out of there by himself? Not to mention, in broad daylight?

Unless....A spark zapped through her mind. One she'd have to mull over, until sharing it with Detective McGuire.

For Diane, the logic of it immediately weakened the grand theft theory as the motive. No, something else was at play. Something sinister and way more grandiose. Murder. Was it pre-meditated murder, for the sake of murder? What had Arabella ever done to deserve a ploy dreamed up by a master thinker to do her in?

If so, mistakes had been made by many evil master thinkers. There'd be some little screw up, some minor detail that would expose it all for what it was. From there, she'd need to provide absolute proof. The kind that held up in a trial, too. Without a witness or an official valid, true confession, she'd need concrete evidence and certainty that placed the killer at the scene at the time of death. Or else, she and the local D.A. would consider her work sloppy. Circumstantial evidence wasn't an option. She resolved to catch the mastermind's mistake.

The next day, she ran all this by McGuire. He seemed pleased, even supportive.

"Do you ever sleep?" he asked lightly, taking off his jacket and slinging it over his shoulder. She'd caught him just before he was scheduled for a meeting with the mayor.

Diane half smirked. "I sleep better when things are tied up... and when Tom's home."

McGuire gave her a high five. "I know the feeling, except the part about Tom. Unsolved cases chip away at me. You'd think I'd weigh less by now."

Diane gave him the laugh he deserved. "How're the mayor and your chief this week?"

McGuire replied, "Still pressing, but hopeful. The Laurens family put up a reward yesterday. Twenty K."

Diane widened her eyes. "I hope it'll make a difference."

"Phone's been ringing again," he said. "Oh, an update: Forensics couldn't get a urine sample. Too much time, too much snow melt."

"Unsurprising, I guess."

"We exhaust every possibility around here. Anything new?"

"And I got to thinking last night about timing and opportunity. Seems to me that during the delivery of the art, the outside doors were open, the studio was unlocked, and later you found the open window. That's open access."

"Granted by Arabella for delivery of the art by the drivers."

"Well, here's a thought. Adam Perinsky, the fly shop guy, was emptying his trash and saw two guys leave in the van."

"Correct. You have quite a memory for names."

She waved it off. "But he didn't see them get out of the van, go inside, and deliver the painting, did he?"

Detective McGuire gazed at her intently. "Nope. Where are you going with this?"

Diane replied, "Well, I was playing 'What if' again. It can open the door to a zillion possibilities."

McGuire hiked an eyebrow. "*What if* we have enough of those right now?"

She ignored his sarcasm. "But do we have the right ones? The ones that count. Ones based on timing and opportunity, and that the Monet was too big for the murderer to leave with?"

"Go on."

"So, what if he had help?"

McGuire sighed. "How the hell did that happen?"

"I don't know...yet."

He leaned forward. "Here's what's bugging me. Along those lines, why would a guy leave a thirty plus million-dollar painting behind in the first place?"

"Maybe finding it there came as a surprise? When he found it, he wasn't equipped to leave with it?" Instinct told her this was an off-the-wall theory, but she threw it out there anyway.

McGuire whistled. "Must've been frustrating for him not to walk away from it. The only witness for a theft of it was dead."

Diane got up, paced around her chair and stopped. "I'm now leaning toward pre-meditated murder. Too messy for grand theft. Unplanned, or whatever. Gut level. It's all I got."

"You think all over the map, don't you?"

"Exhausting possibilities, thanks."

"But we found the Monet in place. It appeared like no attempt was made to move it at all."

"So, I'm thinking a thief isn't what we're after here, Detective McGuire. Somebody wanted Arabella Laurens dead. That was his goal." McGuire showed signs of agreement. "But why, and why then?"

McGuire's phone rang. He leaned on his desk. "Sure," he answered first. "Put him through." He gestured for Diane to sit. "Hello, Sergeant Newberry. Yeah, I've got a minute."

Diane sat and watched McGuire. First, she loved people watching in general. She enjoyed studying their expressions, movements, their stances, their whole persona and body language. She could do it anywhere, too. The practice also sharpened her observation skills. At the moment, McGuire shot to full alert. Straight up spine, fully focused, and avoiding eye contact with her while he spoke with the caller.

Newberry? Morgan Newberry, she processed. Yes, James had mentioned him in regards to his work and connection to fighting crime.

McGuire said, "How about now?" This time he threw Diane a quick glance. She folded her hands on her lap. The tone in his voice was tinged with excitement.

McGuire hung up. "You have an hour or so?"

Diane leaned forward. "The day is mine for how I wish it to be," she said matter-of-factly, "That's the beauty of autonomy and working independently."

The detective visibly reflected on that for about three nanoseconds and said, "Not my style, but that was Morgan Newberry, forensics investigator from the lab in Springs. He's bringing us the painting for James Boyd to store in his lock-up. Thought you might like to be here for the hand-off. He'll give us a full report on his findings."

Diane issued a solid, "Yes." Her heart even thumped a little. She'd get to see another Monet. Even if it were damaged with its telltale paint spatters, it'd be a thrill. She'd also have a stellar opportunity to make her own observations, ask questions, and snap a few photos.

"Good," McGuire said. "I'm calling Mr. Boyd." He tapped in another number.

Diane excused herself and found a vending machine. She punched buttons for a granola bar. She'd missed breakfast and needed to be on her toes for meeting Newberry. Having some fresh air called to her. She stepped outside and ambled over to the rental car.

"Good morning," someone called to her from the pavement.

Looking in that direction, she didn't recognize the man standing there with his dog. She waved out of politeness. "Good morning."

"Say, are you the lady investigator who's trying to find out who killed my house sitter?"

Diane tilted her head with instant interest and took in his appearance. She estimated he was in his early sixties. He had gray hair, wore a navy sweater with loose leather buttons and a pork pie hat with fishing tackle in the brim. She wasn't up for shouting out to each other in the parking lot, so she stepped toward the passerby. His dog wriggled against the leash.

Concerned about transparency, she introduced herself and asked him his name. "I'm Jake Fields. I'm retired, but used to own the jerky shop. Sold it three years ago, after my wife died."

"I'm sorry for your loss."

"I am, too," he said, and looked down at his pooch. "Sparky and I still miss her, don't we, Sparky?" The dog looked up at him with bright eyes. He was obviously enjoying his walk.

Diane asked, "You knew Arabella Laurens?"

"Yes, ma'am. She house sat for me when I went up to Blue Mesa last fall. Very distressed to hear of her death," he said, shaking his head. "Don't know what this world's coming to."

Diane understood his sentiment.

"Last time Arabella sat for me, she left one of her scarves. I wanted to return it to her, but had to leave town for Cheyenne. My brother lives up there, and he was having trouble with his heart. So, Sparky and I stayed with him for a while, didn't we, Sparky?"

Diane checked the dog again. A short-haired spunky kind of dog with grey splotches all over him. Coal-black eyes and nose. Jake had tied a blue bandana around his little neck. The tip of it trailed on the ground.

"Well, Jake," she began, "did you ever feel like Arabella was in some kind of trouble?" She didn't expect much of an answer, but he seemed a grandfatherly type of local guy. The victim might've confided something to him. Something of interest?

Jake took a step closer. "Only once. She seemed mostly a happy sort and did a good job watching my place before and after she was done with work. I'd be gone for four days. She left the place cleaner than I did! And there was food in the refrigerator when I came back. So, I've really lost a good person to watch my place, dang it."

Diane's curiosity piqued. "What kind of trouble had she mentioned?"

Jake said, "Hold on. Over there's a bench. Want to have a seat? My leg's bothering me."

"Sure," she answered, and they headed to the wrought iron bench near a tree.

Settled, Jake went on. "I think it was about a matter of the heart. Personal, lady stuff, you know. She wasn't very old, still single, in her thirties, I think. Parents weren't here. Brother lives in Denver. Pam over at the jewelry store and she'd kept good company. They probably shared a lot of laughs and tears. That's how women friends are." He thought for a second. "Same with my Mildred. She and her church friends were thick as thieves. 'Course I have my angler pals. We meet up at the Elks every Thursday. We have ladies' nights, too. So, if you—"

"Jake, how about you tell me about Arabella's problem?"

The man gazed skyward, as if gathering his thoughts. "A man tried to hustle her, and she didn't like it much. Happened at one of those Art Society meetings. One was held here in town, and after it was over, she'd come over to pick up my key the night before my last fishing trip. She was all in a dither. Not because of the rain, but because he was pushy, not a gentleman."

"Was he local?" Sam Crawford was coming to her mind. He'd been hard to dissuade.

"I don't think so."

"What makes you say that?"

"I asked her what he looked like and she said he was wearing spurs. *Nobody* around here would wear 'em."

Spurs? Diane closed her eyes and reopened them. On a personal note, she was grateful.

"Well, Jake, thanks for this," Diane said, adding it to her mental notes.

"One more thing," he said. "She said he was chewing t'baccy."

"Oh." She grimaced. That could be a turn-off to any woman. "She say anything else?"

Jake thought some more. "It was a dinner dance, and she'd made the mistake of dancing with him and letting him walk her to her car. And that's when he tried to feel her up."

Diane lowered her gaze. "Oh." The unpleasant image rose in her mind.

"Sorry ma'am, that's man talk," Jake said. "It upset her but good. I got to run now. Sparky's going to the spa."

Diane reached down and patted the little dog's head. "You have a good time."

Jake gave him a piece of jerky and off they went. She turned to go back into the police building. *Jerky.* Suddenly, she remembered Pam saying she'd seen the van that delivered the art to Arabella had stopped to pick up someone coming out of the jerky shop on their way down Manitou Avenue, which lead in and out of town. Perhaps one of the two delivery guys had a yearning for jerky. Otherwise, who else could that have been?

Fourteen

Monet

Diane shook Sgt. Newberry's hand. His was a brisk, all-business shake. The gray suit and white shirt made him look more official somehow. No tie needed. His deep-set blue eyes were full of resolve. Another lab guy helped him carry the Monet into James' workroom, where framing normally took place for the gallery. They carefully placed it on a long table and James turned on all the lights.

Everyone stopped moving for a few moments, taking in the painting's awesome presence. Morgan stood at the head of the table, and James stood on his right by the table with Diane next to him on his left. McGuire and Pete Woodrow stood next to each other on the other long side.

Overwhelmed with its beauty, Diane spoke first, softly. "This is such a pleasure. The colors...oh my." She pulled out her phone. "May I?" she asked Newberry. He nodded his approval. "No flash, though."

McGuire leaned down closer to the surface. "I like the water... amazing how he did it with those strokes, short ones, one almost on top of another. So many of them."

Pete held his hat in respect over his heart and shook his head. "Can you imagine knowing him? What a triumph."

All the while, Morgan stood quietly straight and looked reserved; even preoccupied.

Conversely, James was having trouble breathing. He, more than most, understood the effort and value of what everyone was admiring. "How tragic, those paint spatters ruining this masterpiece."

McGuire shot Morgan a glance. "Yes, what about those spots? What's your take on those?"

"The substance on the canvas matches the substance found in the victim's right hand. Fresh oil paint. She squeezed a tube, the top popped off, and paint flew."

Diane looked over at him. "You must be thrilled as the rest of us to have this pass through your hands."

Morgan cleared his throat. "Not so much."

Incredulous, Diane swung her full gaze at him. "Why?" she asked point blank. "Monet was a world master painter. His impressionistic work is considered almost reverent."

James put in, "Yes, how can you *not* be excited?"

Diane sensed Morgan was just getting warmed up and switched her phone on to Record.

Morgan lifted his glasses to the top of his head and let them sit there. "Because, my dear folks, this painting is *not* a Monet. Unfortunately, we're looking at a Rouarde Clementi."

"Excuse me?" James cried, clearly affronted.

"Sorry to disappoint, but this is an authentic Rouarde Clementi. Quite a nice job, actually, for a reproduction."

McGuire and Pete exchanged shocked glances. "You're saying this painting is a fake?"

"A bonafide well-done fake," Morgan confirmed.

Diane collected her wits. "How have you come to this conclusion, Mr. Newberry?"

Everyone could've heard a pin drop. "First, my specialty is art identification. With this piece of evidence, I began with the basics. I assessed the credibility of the painting using high-tech microscopes, radiology, and infrared equipment. Each tell me their own story. I also have honed a keen familiarity with the artist's style and studied the materials used during the periods he'd painted and his changing themes. Monet's one of my favorites."

James interceded. "He was very prolific."

"True, and I ran into trouble early on this one. For example, see this section of the blue water?" He used a light pen to indicate where he was talking about. A bright red dot settled close to Monet's signature in the lower right-hand corner.

"Apparently, Ms. Laurens had begun work there, so I followed up in that spot where a dot of white canvas shows through. She'd removed a tiny loose microchip for color analysis, so she could match its color perfectly. Standard procedure. Nothing else counts as much as *perfect* in art restoration, just saying." He turned off the pen.

"That was as far as she got. I believe she was murdered at that point." He paused. "I can't help wondering what she'd thought during her color matching process. The computer screen we found provided the name of the color she'd run through for identification. If it was off...and it was...she probably was curious and wanted to do a retry. If she'd had the time to rerun it, she was about to have a true Aha! moment. A big red flag was on its way to the ground at the goal line."

Diane and the rest of the group stood transfixed.

"In more than one way," Pete soon interjected into the quiet.

James offered, "Arabella loved his blues. Blue was her special interest...there's a progression in its generational and historical development and use. She could name blues spot on." He pointed at the canvas. "Looks to me like that area on the canvas is several shades of blue. So, I'm not surprised she started there."

"That and repair work was needed there," Morgan added.

James said, "She could do both...clean and repair. Each process requires great expertise. She'd once shared, 'My goal is to have a painting regain its original brightness and beauty.' And she got good at it."

Diane said, "I'm sure her goal was no different for this one. It was special."

McGuire asked simply, "So, exactly what was wrong?"

"Yes, what was the tipoff?" Woodrow wanted to know.

Morgan continued. "Good questions. You see, we know that Monet used nine colors in his work. Leadwhite, chrome yellow, cadmium yellow, viridian green, emerald green, French ultramarine, cobalt blue, madder red, and vermillion. He dropped using earth tones, brown, black after 1886. He usually used pigments right out of the tube. Mixing colors happened on the canvas. He never painted over top another work; he didn't have to. X-raying this canvas confirmed such was the case here. This water lily painting was likely part of the series he'd begun in 1914. And it's different. It's vertical."

Diane admired Morgan. He was a force to reckon with. He'd bridged art and science in an analytical, forensic way. Fascinating. Crucial. A lifetime work.

"But to answer your questions, I ran a mass spectrometry analysis myself and discovered that the microchip of paint wasn't cobalt or French ultramarine. It's, in fact, Azure. See how much of it was used in that section?"

"A lot," Diane said, peering closely at the beautiful water.

McGuire opened his hands. "And?"

"Azure wasn't invented in the color world until nineteen thirty-two. Also, there's no lead present on this canvas. At one time lead in paint was common. But not today. Another point is that underdrawings are present for this painting."

Diane asked, "What're they?"

"Those are light preparation markings the artist makes first on the canvas to arrange what goes where. They're common for artists to use, but Monet used few, or none."

"How d'you know what's under there?" McGuire asked, pointing to the surface.

"Infrared reflectography penetrates paint to 'see' what visible light can't. Another thing, Monet was right-handed. We know that from videos made of him painting in his garden.

"But many brush strokes here were painted by a left-handed person. We can tell the direction they go from the brush pressure applied at one end of the stroke, or the base, and how the end of the stroke differs. It's as if strokes were painted backwards. Monet didn't play games with his strokes, but Rouarde Clementi did."

"He risked taking license. Self-indulgent," James noted.

"Clementi's classic trademark," Morgan said.

"Where is this Clementi guy?" Pete Woodrow said and puffed his chest.

Morgan smiled broadly. "Colorado Corrections Center, Denver."

"Amen," James said resolutely. "How did he operate?"

"Like most unscrupulous black market and dark web sellers," McGuire provided.

"So that's how Walter Stonehaven added this fine fake to his collection?"

"Seems so."

"I don't buy this at all," James said emphatically. "My sense is that he is a purist."

Nick stepped in. "Museums and galleries are known to purposefully show forgeries, for various reasons."

"Mine doesn't," James huffed.

"Nonetheless, there's a market for them."

Pete shook his head. "Who cares about having a fake cleaned?"

"Why not?" McGuire intervened, playing Devil's Advocate. "They get dirty, too."

"Great. Dirty art, all way around," Pete said. "What else?" he asked Nick Morgan.

Morgan resumed, "Monet's strokes were honest, simple, and when put together, they made up a whole. When we're close like this, we can see each one. When we stand back, our eyes perceive them as color field units...in this case, water and water lilies. He painted around two hundred fifty waterlily canvases. None of them look the same."

"You sure know a lot about this," Pete Woodrow said, scratching his eyebrow.

"I'm paid to," Morgan said. "Moreover, Monet broke what he saw down to swashes or dashes of color. He could see yellow in green, and pink in blue. Very few hard edges...softness, simplified impressions of what was in front of him. He also saw basic shapes. A roof was a rectangle, a square a cottage, and a cylinder with a dome on top created a haystack."

Diane nodded, still lost in Newberry's verbal report. Her next thought popped out of her mouth, "Then, Arabella suspected this was a fake."

"It's my guess she had early clues. She *had* to."

"But she couldn't act on them," Diane concluded. "Someone interrupted her."

James' voice shook. "Does Walter Stonehaven know this?"

McGuire replied, looking at his watch. "He will in another hour."

Diane's heart went out to Walter and Ruth. Aside from their kids and home, their art collection was their pride and joy. How invaded they were going to feel.

"What about the painting's provenance? Doesn't that check out?"

"I've not been privy to it. Mr. Stonehaven has the history of its creation and ownership in his possession."

James slapped his hand on the table. "How'd this happen? Sotheby's wouldn't sell him a fake, for God's sake!"

"Selling one is what makes it a forgery," Diane slid in. "Fraudulent."

"Whatever. I'm sure Mr. Stonehaven bought this in good faith, and Sotheby's sold it to him in good faith."

Exactly, crossed Diane's busy mind. *So, how did it end up in Walter's hands?*

Morgan said, "I might add that art forgery isn't unusual. At one time, young art students copied the greats until they got good enough to produce fine reproductions. Then they were accepted and painted in their own styles. Picasso was most forged; Salvatore Dali comes in second. He signed canvases for shared profits."

McGuire whistled. "Anything else for us, Sergeant Newberry?"

"Done," Morgan said and handed McGuire his report. "Except to say, you've got some work cut out for you." He gestured with his thumb toward the art. "Keep this locked up. Good luck."

Diane stood stock still. *Luck?* This kind of food for thought super charged her brain. A vague picture of her own was beginning to form. No luck involved. Only greed and mistakes...

Fifteen

Somebody Likes Jerky

The time had come for Diane to explore Jake's Jerky Shop. The next morning, she waited until 10:00 a.m. and ambled into the shop where a counter person named Richard greeted her.

"G'morning, ma'am. Nice morning."

"Yes, it is."

"Might even get up to fifty-five today," he said and straightened a stack of coupons by the cash register. "Are you interested in some jerky? We finished a fresh batch of alpaca this morning."

Diane held back a grimace. *Alpacas are way too cute to eat.* She stepped further in, glancing at the racks holding plastic bags of assorted jerky. She was impressed with how many kinds there were as she approached the counter. Customers could choose from elk, beef, buffalo, duck, and others. She wondered if Tom would want some alligator jerky, but cast aside the idea, as lately he was getting more into eating fish. Besides, she was here on business, so didn't feel the need to buy.

"I'm pretty sure I'm not," she said apologetically. The mixed aromas like smoky and pepper in the shop were a bit much for her. "First, I've met Jake Fields who used to own this shop. He told me of this place and he gives his dog jerky."

Richard stepped from around the counter. "Yes, he's highly regarded around here. Better than many. He knew when to fold his cards. His favorite is our bison jerky. His dog Sparky likes good old beef the best. Maybe your dog would like some? Wait, I'll give you a sample."

Diane put up her hand to stop him. "I don't have a dog, thanks. So you hold on to that sample." Personally, she didn't want to touch the brown strips. The scent was so strong, she'd be having dogs following her all the way back up on Columbine Path. "I'm here about another matter of great importance."

Richard straightened and smoothed the front of his burgundy leather vest. His dark hair almost touched the collar. He had pierced ears and looked like maybe he played in a band somewhere at night. A tattoo of a fancy guitar and a pick took up space on his lower forearm. A Guns 'n Roses t-shirt blasted her eyes with black, red, and gray.

"My boss is Harley Clark. Would you like to speak to him?"

Diane nodded. "That'd be nice, thanks."

Richard hesitated, and unabashedly looked her over. Jeans and a dark T-shirt with a navy-blue sweatshirt over top had been her choices for comfort today. "But I don't think we have any job openings for now."

Diane assured him, "I have a job, thanks." She gave him one of her cards. "This is about Arabella Laurens."

Richard's expression fell serious and concern flickered in his hazel eyes. "Oh...that's the poor woman who died some time back."

"Murdered."

A silent beat followed. "I read about it. I'll get Harley for you."

Harley came forth from out of the back of store. He was heavyset and wore wire glasses perched on his nose. Tufts of white hair hugged his head over his ears. He smiled and shook Diane's hand. "What can I help you with?"

"I have a few questions...about the day that one of your locals, Ms. Laurens, passed away."

Harley hiked an eyebrow. "Terrible thing. She was a customer at Christmas."

"Well, I'm hoping you'll be able to help me."

The shop owner swept his gaze over the front counter and at the front door. Two guys were on their way inside. "Come. We can go over by the coffee mugs to talk."

He led the way to a far corner where a display of mugs filled pegs jutting out from the wooden wall. Horseshoes, lariats, and cowboy hat décor made it more Western country. They settled at a small table near a painting of a cowboy eating jerky on his horse and a Charles Russell print of open landscape with cattle.

"Am not sure why you've come to see us, but I'll help however I can," Harley said.

"Well, I'm here about a certain customer who came in here the morning she died. So, I'm wondering if, perhaps, you or one of your clerks might remember helping him."

Harley locked gazes with her. He looked a bit lost. "You know that all happened three months ago."

"January seventh, to be exact. But sometimes folks remember things, and I thought it worthwhile to check. Maybe there was something unusual about that morning that stuck in somebody's mind?"

Harley pulled closer to the table. "January seventh. The good thing is that it happened during our post-Christmas lull. Fewer customers, you see. The bad thing is that I had extra temporary help then due to taking inventory, and they're not here now."

"Any chance I'd get to view what was recorded on a security camera that day?"

Harley leaned back. "No chance, actually. I just had a system put in last month. Our inventory was coming up short, so now I'm fighting fire with fire. How about we get Richard over here? He's my regular counter person. He remembers things like who likes what kind of jerky and when they were in last. Kind of like a barkeep who stores tabs up here." He tapped his head.

Diane grew hopeful. Of sharp interest for her was Pam's report of how she had seen the same van that had delivered the artwork at the Falcon Building briefly stop here at the jerky shop. Diane guessed since their work was done for the day after delivering the Monet to Arabella, they had time on their hands. As there's a lot to see and do in Manitou Springs, it wasn't surprising they had done some things before leaving town, like picking up jerky. For now, mining Richard's memory seemed the best bet for trying to learn more.

"Yes, a moment with Richard, please."

She gazed out the window while Harley went to get him. The whole surface of that morning seemed like it needed more scratching. In some ways, Diane felt like an archaeologist extracting bone fragments, piece by piece, from ancient dry dirt. Eager to find the next piece, she pulled her notepad out from her bag as Richard took Harley's place at the small table.

"Ahh, we meet again," he began with a half-smile. "I might have something for you."

~ * ~

The next day Diane burst into Detective McGuire's office.

"Good morning," she chirped and stopped dead in her tracks.

McGuire held his hand up for her to be quiet. Now.

"*Whose* print?" he almost shouted into the phone. "Well, get on it, then!"

Clearly irritated, he spoke first. "Forensics found unidentified fingerprints on one of the one hundred-dollar bills left at the victim's studio."

Diane backed up a bit and gaped. "Good. Do you have a few minutes?" She presented him with a bag of jerky.

"For that, no," he growled. "It's not even ten o'clock yet."

"It's from Harley Clark. He sends his regards."

Detective McGuire leveled his gaze on her. "So...you've been to the jerky store."

Diane pulled out a chair and sat. "You might want to put your phone on hold."

McGuire tapped a button. "What's up?" He folded his hands together on the desk top and gave her his attention.

Diane pulled out her notes. "I have something."

"Not measles, I hope."

Diane widened her eyes. Roger McGuire could certainly change moods on a dime.

"I talked again with Pam last evening on the phone. She'd reported to me that she'd seen the plain van that had delivered the Monet to Arabella's studio parked by the loading dock that morning of January seven. She also knew what it was for, and was excited about it, because Arabella would be letting her have a peek at a Monet up close. This was as she was opening up for the day."

"Okay."

"Pam also mentioned that about two hours later, she'd also seen the van slow up by Jake's Jerky and somebody get in and they drove off."

"What's significant about that?"

"A lot. Last night I asked her if she got a good glimpse at the guy who was getting into the van. She explained because of the distance she didn't, except she could tell he was wearing a dark hat."

McGuire's eyes lit up. "The dude who Sam saw peeing in the alley?"

"My guess is, yes. But there's more. I've had a nice chat with Richard Glowinksi, the counter guy at Jake's. I asked him about the day Arabella died, January seventh, and if he remembered anything about business that morning. Sure enough, he tagged it because that was the first day of the shop's quarterly inventory. Apparently, Harley put him in charge of tallying the stock in the front end. So Richard organized a team of temps to get the job done."

McGuire reached for his mug. "You want some coffee?"

"Sure," she said and went on while he swiveled his chair around to the credenza behind and poured her a cup. "Richard sat across from me and scratched his head with a pencil and then rolled his fingers on the top of the little table where we sat by a window. I just gave him plenty of time and space. No use rushing mining a gold vein, right?"

"I'm not a prospector, but I see your point."

She sipped from the hot brew. "Well, he remembers a guy coming into the shop and asking one of the inventory team about some jerky hanging on a rack. The kid told him he'd have to ask Richard about it, that they were just there taking inventory. The customer kind of got huffy and said he was in a hurry, which Richard overheard. Richard went to help and they started over."

She fell quiet for a moment and lifted pages of notes and stopped.

"Richard says the guy bought about eight pounds of jerky. Assorted, you see. Richard was happy for the sale, because this was right after the holidays and business was falling dead. Anyway, the guy pays for the jerky with a one-hundred dollar bill. Which is what triggered Richard's memory. That and one other thing."

"Was he wearing a dark hat?"

"Yep."

McGuire shook his head. "That's it?"

"Nope."

McGuire flashed her a big patronizing smile. "Well, what happened then?" His tone was growing surly again. He truly was having a morning.

Diane looked up at him. "See, that's where it gets *interesting*. Richard said—"

"Want to tell me why, Ms. Phipps? Or will this be twenty-one questions?"

Diane pressed her lips together and gave it a minute. "There were three men in the van who delivered the painting, not just the two couriers we knew about."

McGuire raised his eyebrows. "That is *interesting*. How'd you find that out?"

"Richard said the jerky dude left a bag of it on the counter. Richard tagged after him to give it to him. He reached him at the van, and two guys were sitting in the front eating hot dogs from The Arcade, and the customer loaded himself in the back and they took off."

McGuire took a minute to process. "Who's the third guy?"

"The guy Sam saw in the alley? The murderer?" she asked quietly. "And where was he from?"

It was all she could say at the moment. There were too many unanswered questions and insufficient evidence to point the finger at anyone. But, this much she knew: more than what met the eye was going on.

Questions exploded. Had the third guy paid Arabella a visit? If so, when, how, and what was his role in this sordid affair? Was he the last person to see her alive instead of the two couriers? Did the couriers know he'd seen her? What was her relationship to him? Was he a secret enemy?

For Diane, the stranger was becoming a person of interest... moving fast toward being a prime suspect. He'd certainly found his window of opportunity. Arabella was alone. The timing was perfect... if he had murder on his mind.

Sixteen

Aunt Meredith Calls

Diane cooked a late lunch for herself and gave Walter's budget a break. The kitchen in the rental cottage was completely serviceable. She wasn't used to cooking with gas but liked it by the time she'd finished making potatoes and a burger in a cast iron Lodge pan. While tearing lettuce for a salad, she mulled over what she had jumped into with this case. Momentum was building, which pleased her. However, questions still stirred, which fired her to find more answers.

Discovering three men had been on the scene the morning Arabella was killed intrigued her. One thing often led to another, and she was eager to see where this new tip would take her.

Her memory served up how Willow had encountered a conversation in the stable between Walter and his horse guy, Rydell. Since he didn't want to participate, had Walter found another ride-along soft security man to do the job?

Suddenly, Diane felt sorry for Walter. He was a victim, too. He'd lost a painting, even though it was surprisingly fake, which left much more to sort out on what had happened to the authentic one. A woman died while working on one of his possessions. Now, had he unwittingly added a possible murderer to the delivery team?

Diane's cell phone rang, and she took the call.

"Hi, Aunt Meredith," she greeted with a smile. "How're you doing?"

"Pretty good. More snow comes tomorrow, and I'm thinking about moving to Florida. Have had enough, thank you. Besides that, I'm wondering how're you coming along with your investigations?"

Diane suppressed a sigh. "I'm hard at it, is all I can say for now. Each week I get closer to the situation and the people and how the investigation team here thinks and acts, and I can't share a lot right now, but some things are coming to light, and...I'm missing Tom."

Aunt Meredith offered her sweet consolations, and added, "I'm getting more worried about my friend, Yves St. Vrain. I was hoping to give him some encouraging news when he comes over for dinner tomorrow evening. He's still very wrought about the painting. He reminded me he's only weeks away from retiring and doesn't want to go out of the work force like this...with this big black spot, like a ruined Monet, on his career. And a murder."

Diane raised her eyebrows. "How'd you know it was ruined, Aunt Merrie?"

"From Walter. A detective McGill, or something like that, called him the other day to update him on what was found. Apparently, the painting that poor woman was working on was a fake. Now, isn't that the pits? Walter suffers from anxiety and sorrow. Ruth isn't much better. So, it's a challenge up here right now. And, Yves is wound up tighter than a top! He gets red talking about it all and is going to have a heart attack."

Diane closed her eyes. She sorely wished she had good news to offer, some that would give relief. But she needed to sit on what was forming in her mind. More time was needed and more chance for information to surface. So, she played her social call cards close to her chest.

"Just everyone needs to hang in a bit longer. We're all doing our best."

"Oh, I know you are," Aunt Meredith assured. "But just hearing your voice helps to calm my own worry for them."

Diane smiled. "Sweet of you. You can tell Yves and Walter that the truth always rises and it will here, too."

Aunt Meredith coughed and cleared her throat. "Well, for Yves' sake, and Walter's," she rasped, "I'm hoping it's not more ugly truth."

Diane paused. "No promises, Aunt Merrie. I'm sorry. I know Yves is your friend. It's good of you to follow up with him. Best thing you can do for him is *listen,* for now."

"True. I guess he just wants to know if you're closer to figuring this out. He needs peace."

"The answer is yes, I'm closer," she offered. "But not close enough to apprehend anybody yet." She squeezed in a drink of water. "Maybe Yves will feel better when he meets me at the Front Range Art Society party. It's this coming Saturday night, and I've been invited."

"I'm sure he will," Aunt Meredith said with relief. "Thank you."

"Have you heard from Tom?"

Aunt Meredith softened her voice. "No, nothing, dear. If it helps, I hear there's a good candy store where you are, and they have great saltwater taffy...for a touch of home."

Diane's voice caught as she said, "Thank you."

Another moment passed and Diane said goodbye and turned to her burger and looking at the pine trees out the kitchen window. Despite daylight saving time just beginning, it still got dark early in March. At the moment, the sun coated the pine needles with amber light, making the scenery somewhat surreal. Especially for her, as she was used to seeing palm fronds out the kitchen window.

Oh, how Diane suddenly missed the ocean. Still, the mountain terrain offered its own beauty. Seeing Pikes Peak every day awed her. The pine boughs lofted in the breeze and fell gently again, beckoning her outdoors.

Thinking of it, a short walk would do her good. She'd been doing brain crunches since she got here. "Time to breathe," she told herself.

After finishing her food, she put on her walking shoes, hoping they'd suffice. Days ago she'd spotted a trail head further up the hill. It'd be close to home, and she'd only do an hour round-trip. A laughable hike effort probably to the locals, but it'd be enough for her to let her head coast and to take in the warmer air that was reappearing. Relaxing could clear the clutter in her thoughts. Who knew what clarity would come forth? Clarity brought answers and plans.

Her next chance to somewhat chill would be at the Hotel Eleganté for the F.R.A.S. party. James was kind to invite her so she could be part of Arabella's social world for a few hours. It was still work, but she was looking forward to dressing up.

Twenty minutes later, Diane found herself on a narrow dirt trail with tall trees and thick brush on either side. The views between the trees were stupendous as she walked up the trail, and up and up. She'd passed a few couples who were coming down and everyone waved.

Just ahead was a small scenic view area. She headed toward the big rocks that offered a resting place. She'd even packed a water bottle and sipped after she came to a halt. She did feel on top of the world.

Aside from a remarkable vantage point, with a fall-away scenic slope below, rocks, pine needles, pine cones, branches, and red dirt formed a ribbon through the trees below. The ocean never gave her this kind of feeling, and she took her time to soak it all up. She wished Tom were here to enjoy it with her. When she found something special like this, her first inclination was to share it with him. It always felt selfish to keep it all to herself.

The light was fading, so she went to turn back. She heard branches crunching below and stepped over to the edge of the graded dirt area and stood still, hoping to catch a glimpse of some wildlife. Yet, nothing but more trees and brush met her search.

It was then that she sensed someone rushing at her from behind. A blur of dark...She turned her head for better peripheral vision, but the wrong way. A solid body slam against her back threw her off-balance. Forward and down she fell...over the edge.

Rolling and bumping, Diane soon crumpled to a stop. Moaning, she lay on her back and brushed dirt from her face. Everything wobbled around her. Nausea tugged at her. She struggled to pull her cell phone from her jacket pocket and shakily punched 9-1-1. Her heart pounded in her ears, and she could hardly talk. "Help..."

Her head throbbed, and all went dark.

Seventeen

After the Hike

Diane opened her eyes slowly. Three concerned pairs of eyes were staring at her. They belonged to Detective McGuire, James, and Pam. A nurse held her hand.

"Good, she's awake," McGuire announced.

She blinked and looked around. "What's going on?"

A nurse replied, "You took a nasty spill. You're in Penrose."

Pam's blue eyes looked moist. "You fell, honey, off the White Eagle trail."

James shook his head. "Good to see you. We need to chat about hiking alone."

Detective McGuire took it from there. "You are one damn lucky woman, Ms. Phipps. No broken bones, no cracked ribs or head or jaw."

"You still have all your teeth," James said.

"And you're alive," Pam said.

Diane noticed the bruise on the back of her hand and managed a smile. Her body ached. "That's the good news, right? But I look pretty bad, right?"

James answered, "I'm afraid so, yes. Bruises and a scratch on your cheek."

Pam came in second. "No, you look just fine. Maybe like you just got up, but...otherwise fine." Her eyes twinkled with relief. "Nothing a little make-up can't fix."

McGuire closed with, "You look like what's to be expected from falling down a rugged slope. Scraped up here and there. You're in here for observation."

She lifted her hands to her head. Her fingers touched the soft gauze bandage that covered her forehead and circled round back. Overall, she knew she wasn't a bad looking chick, but she dreaded looking in the mirror right now. Why vanity was hitting her, she didn't know. Someone kindly hung a towel over the mirror hanging on the wall by the window. It was pitch dark outside.

"How long have I been here?"

"It's nine-thirty," Pam said, looking at her watch.

"Almost four hours," McGuire added. "Want to tell us what happened? You tripped over what?"

"Was it a snake?" Pam said, making a face. "Happened to me once."

Diane shook her head from side to side while James poured her some water. She accepted the glass with a shaky hand. "Well, I just wanted to walk, you know. It helps me sort things out, and I'd seen that trail up the road from where I'm staying. I figured I had about an hour of daylight left and took off. That's about it, except there were some snow patches, but I walked around them and kept going."

McGuire scratched his eyebrow. She couldn't quite tell what he was thinking, but went on.

"There's a neat little scenic spot up there with a sign, and I stopped there. Gorgeous. Anyway, I was about to leave to come back down when I heard a noise coming from down below the slope. I was hoping for a bear, or something. Or maybe a deer, or a Rocky Mountain big horn sheep."

"No sheep, not here," James put in.

"And that's when I felt something coming at me..." She lifted her hands to her eyes. "Just a blur...and so fast...body slammed my back, and it took the wind out of me. I flew forward...over...the edge."

All three people's mouths fell open.

Detective McGuire recovered first, which didn't surprise her, since he dealt with nasty deeds all the time. "You're saying you were *pushed*?"

"More like blasted," Diane recalled, beginning to feel anger burn inside.

"Oh, for God's sake," James exclaimed.

Pam's eyes widened in disbelief. "Pushed?"

A knock landed on the door as it pushed gently open. All turned toward it. Maria stepped inside and quickly walked to Diane's bedside. "Oh, my gosh," she said. "I heard you had a mishap and couldn't get here until now. Florine's house is nearest the trail, and she said she'd seen you being hauled downhill on a stretcher! How are you? I couldn't wait until morning. What happened?"

Pam filled her in. From the looks of it, they knew each other, too.

Maria wrung her hands. "Well, if there's anything you need, just let me know. I'm right next door, and it's no bother." She opened her boho bag and handed Diane a white envelope. "Here, I saw this under the windshield wiper on your rental car. Almost blew off. Thought I'd bring it with me."

Diane thanked her for coming and opened the envelope. Pulling out the contents, she unfolded a piece of plain white paper and read the word aloud. "LEAVE."

"It says *leave*?" James confirmed.

"Oh my. Is that a threat?" Pam asked nervously. "What is happening in this town?"

McGuire stepped closer and plucked the paper from her hand using his thumb and forefinger. "I'll take that," he said authoritatively and pulled an evidence bag from his jacket pocket. Leave it to him to be prepared.

"How soon can I get out of here?" Diane asked the nurse. No fear rattled her voice.

"Where are you going?" James asked.

"To work."

As the minutes passed, Diane was getting more fired up. *Somebody* wanted her off this case. All the more reason for her to stick.

"When the doctor releases you," the nurse said. "Possibly tomorrow, or maybe not."

"Tomorrow. Fine. I've things to do."

"Not so fast," McGuire told her. "Your free-to-move-about-the-cabin days are numbered. I'm putting a suit on you. Bill Schriever... he's the best undercover guy in the county. You'll never know he's around."

Mixed feelings welled up inside Diane. She supposed a "thank you" was in order, but it was tough to take—she'd become a target. Still, she didn't need to be babysat. It wasn't the first time she'd encountered danger. Neither did she need her movement restricted. Spontaneity and serendipity often worked in her favor.

The note proved her hunch was correct. She was getting closer to uncovering the secrets this case held under lock and key. The things that weren't adding up in one way were adding up in another. Walter wouldn't have ever bought a forgery. So, somebody somewhere along the line had to exchange the real Monet for a fake one. When and how did it happen?

~ * ~

Diane left the hospital in Colorado Springs the next afternoon. She made it home on her own. There was a scruffy-looking guy up on a ladder clearing pine needles from the rain gutters. Undoubtedly, he was Undercover Bill, courtesy of Detective McGuire.

Maria had left flowers for her on the front step. She stooped and picked them up while her body complained. She was indeed stiff and sore. She fought the thought she might not be in good enough shape to attend the gala, as it was only three days away. Her bruises wouldn't fade by then, either. But make-up would help, and if she lay low as the doctor suggested, she could at least make a short appearance.

She let herself inside, carried the vase to the table by the window in the kitchen and made some tea. Mug in hand, she went to the side room where her case board stood waiting for more notes.

Diane picked up the marker and wrote in big red letters: INSIDE JOB?

She let her gaze travel over all the names she'd posted. Settling in a comfy overstuffed chair with foxes on it, she stared at the board. Questions bombarded her. Who was involved? Who was the mastermind? Who had something to gain? Who had the *most* to gain?

Who of them wants me out of here?

Eighteen

A Surprise Visit

Friday afternoon rolled around and Diane had about enough of self-recovery. Inertia may be good for her body, but it was fogging her mind. Her phone rang. Just the sound of it held promise for life returning to normal.

"Yes, Detective McGuire?" she answered with anticipation.

"How sore are you?" he asked, sounding congested.

She walked to the living room, this time without one ache. "Am better, thanks. Why?"

"Come on down. A visitor's here to see you...alone," he said. "She's hurting...bring Kleenex. I ran out. Have a cold."

Diane headed for the bedroom to change. "No problem. See you in thirty."

~ * ~

Willow Haverstone visibly relaxed when Diane walked into the storage space Detective McGuire let them use to speak in private.

Whatever was on tearful Willow's mind had set the parameters, and Detective McGuire was flexible enough to go with the flow.

Diane pushed aside her surprise upon seeing Willow there in town. She reached out her hand for a warm shake with the woman, who appeared to be in her late twenties. From reading report notes on the Haverstones, she remembered Willow was a hostess at the golf club and fond of horses.

Diane pulled up a step stool for a seat and set her bag on the floor. Willow was perched on top of a tall stool in front of a mop. A bare lightbulb hung from above. Its low wattage threw shadows over the shelves of cleaning supplies, brushes, and a dust pan.

"It's good to see you again," Diane began. "What's happening, and why are we in here?" she asked gently.

"Because I don't want to cry out there." She pointed out the door and held a small book in her hand. "Do you remember when we were down here and were picking up the rest of Arabella's things?"

Diane nodded. "I know it was a sad time." Going through a homicide victim's personal possessions by friends and family had to be tough for them. Crime scene investigators did it methodically as a matter of course. But taking the deceased's clothes out of the dryer for the last time for packing pulled unparalleled heartstrings.

"Do you remember when I asked for the quilt my mom had given her?"

Diane's memory worked again. "Sure."

Willow dabbed at her eyes with a lace-edged hankie. Despite the tears, she looked healthy and well-dressed in skinny jeans, pastel pink heels, a cropped cream leather jacket, and a white Ann Klein mock turtle neck sweater. Pearl earrings finished off the outfit. "Well, it was a big bundle, and I put it on the chair in my sitting room."

Diane pulled her knees up closer to her chest for comfort. She sensed this was going to take a while and wished she'd brought in a bottle of water. Best thing to do, though, was not rush Willow, as she was connecting with Diane in a sisterly way where girly chat could unfold.

"Okay, and why are you here?" she opened gently. More surprising was that she'd come alone without her fiancé, Leo.

"First, we came down a few days ago, early for the gala tomorrow night. Leo wanted to see some sights like the Cliff Dwellings, I wanted to go to the Cheyenne Mountain Zoo, and Rydell wanted to walk up the Incline. You know, things like that." She leveled her steady gaze on Diane. "I also wanted to do some shopping...and that's where they think I am."

"Shopping."

"Yes, and clearly, I'm not, Ms. Phipps."

Her tone shifted into more formality, which signaled Diane to pull out her small notebook and pen from her bag. "Is this about Arabella?" she ventured.

"Yes," Willow sniffled. "And it's...it's about Leo." Willow again struggled for composure.

Diane reached over and patted her knee. "It's okay; take all the time you need."

Willow lifted her chin. "I—I wanted to see you because...I found this wrapped up inside the quilt. It's a journal, sort of. It belonged to Arabella." She exhaled in a rush and handed the small floral covered book to Diane.

Diane widened her eyes with awe and held it in her hand. She resisted the urge to gorge herself on its pages, hungry for clues, tips, and accountings to help close this case.

"In her handwriting, I believe," Willow finished. "But not every day. There are gaps. Some of it's about her work, like how swirls are sometimes better for cleaning paint than short dabs, and how she couldn't wait to work on the Monet. Some of it's personal, too, like how she felt when James kissed her for the first time, and then later when they...you know," she paused and looked up at the low ceiling, as if searching for help from above. "And...there are words about her brother...Leo, my fiancé." Her frown deepened.

"Disturbing words?" Diane coaxed, suspecting the answer.

"She wrote about how she was beginning to doubt the love of her bother. It really bothered her. One of her last entries is about how Leo had come to see her at her studio, and he told her he didn't want her to marry James."

Diane raised her eyebrows for effect. "How come?"

"She said Leo's been casting shade on him when he was alone with her and had the chance."

"Did she write why he didn't like James?"

"She was trying to figure it out. Leo didn't seem to like how James was in the art business, for one thing. Leo didn't like that James lived here in Manitou Springs away from Denver, for another. He didn't even like it that *she* lived here, either." She shifted positions on the stool and tucked her foot around the bottom rung. "Which I'd have had a fit about if it were me," she added pointedly. "Arabella had her own life, and she was making something of it. Wish I could've gotten to know her better." She brushed a loose hair from her shoulder. "She used turquoise blue ink, my favorite."

Diane smiled. "I wished I could've met her, too. James is still struggling. He invited me to the gala, so I could be part of her art social world for a short while. I'll be glad to meet Yves, your father's curator, and the guy who takes care of the horses."

"Oh, that'd be Rydell Coburn. He's quite good with them, and an excellent blacksmith. My dad met him at a horse sale. Rydell was born in Wyoming, and it's amazing he's here today because when he was six months old, his parents abandoned him. Just up and left."

Nineteen

Evidence

Diane blinked. She'd heard the West could be harsh, like dragging women through cactus for liking someone they shouldn't have, but Rydell's story took the cake. It didn't surprise her that he'd found comfort with horses, who were purportedly smarter than a lot of folks.

"I'll get to meet him, too," Diane said with interest.

"There'll be a small invitational show of some member's art. One of his horseshoe wreaths will be shown. He has a way with metal," she said offhandedly. "We're staying in Springs, and are all going together tomorrow night." She still looked troubled.

"Anything else you want to share?" Diane asked.

"Uh-huh. Arabella was growing curious."

"Of what? Whom?"

"Well, toward the end...I mean before she...died, she wrote about how much Leo, Rydell, and Yves hung out together. They were becoming like brothers, the three of them. She was trying to figure out why, because even though they were connected to my family, they didn't have that much in common. It was a mystery to her. She was even feeling as if she were in competition with them for a bit of her brother's time. Like when Leo and Rydell had to take the estate truck into Denver on an errand for Yves and didn't come back until the next day, which messed up Arabella and Leo's plans to visit the Denver Art Museum. Things like that. And I believe her. More than once, Leo has begged off us doing something together because he'd already slotted time with his two buddies. So, I understand Arabella's frustration."

"Must be true for her to mention it," Diane said, already trying to sort it out.

Willow scrunched up her nose. "They just seemed like an odd lot. Yves is much older than they are and had his own life planned for retirement that would be taking him away from the Stonegate collection."

Diane listened and wrote often.

Could James have interfered with their brotherhood? How so?

"Anyway," Willow continued, "Arabella must not have used the quilt my mother had given her because it was still wrapped with the green grosgrain ribbon. When I opened the quilt the other day, the journal fell out. I didn't know what it was at first. But her name is written inside on the first page. *Arabella Francesca Laurens.*"

She looked down at her finger wrapped with a sizable diamond ring and fell quiet. Diane retraced her own thoughts in the interim. *Francesca?*

"And now I'm not so sure about my Leo," Willow fretted. "I'm wondering what all this means." Another long pause passed. "I just know I'm not built to play second fiddle to my husband's continual need to be with the boys first, or to give my heart to a guy who has lost total regard for his own sister because of whom she wants to marry. Personally, I don't get it. I like James."

Diane concurred and realized that even though she'd met Leo, she didn't know much about him. "How'd you meet Leo?" she asked.

Willow half smiled. "We had worked on the same publicity committee for the Front Range Arts Society Christmas Ball two years ago in Denver. My degree was in marketing, and Leo's was in chemistry and business, and he went on for his MBA. He's doing quite well now," Willow threw in. "His college roommate, Toby, had liked beer. He took it to his own level and set up a micro-brewery. Leo helps him out in the tap room."

"Enterprising, busy people," Diane said.

Willow's eyes brightened. "Leo's not afraid to work, and I admire that in him. If he sees an opportunity that suits him, he goes for it. He wants to retire at age fifty and for us to get a place in the mountains. He loves music and is thinking about opening a recording studio for his second career. Takes a lot of capital for that, but he'll make it."

"Undoubtedly," Diane said.

"Rydell's thinking about throwing in with him. He likes music, too. Plays the guitar."

More notes hit Diane's little notebook. "Is Rydell married?"

"Heavens, no. He's free-range, and likes it that way." She thought for a moment. "I heard he'd hit on Arabella once...in the wrong way. I thought Leo would have words with him, but he didn't. And he should've, you know? Arabella was his *sister!*"

Diane looked up from her pages. Willow's indignance tightened her mouth. Moments of raw truth were hard to take in matters of the heart. This girl was in the midst of sorting out her feelings about her future.

"Everything was so planned for Leo and me," she said, "But now, I'm not so sure I'll be with him. I-I just need to think this through... more time." She looked beseechingly at Diane.

The situation tugged at Diane's heart. She offered gently, "If it helps, it's better to know and live within your limitations. Thank you for bringing me this journal." Somewhat worn, it felt like hot gold in Diane's hand. Tonight she would comb through the whole thing.

Willow nodded. "I didn't read it all...started in the middle, really. When I got to the part about Leo, I stopped."

Twenty

The Help

Diane nodded. "I'm wondering about your father's curator, Yves. When I met your dad at Stonegate about me doing the cleaning, Yves wasn't there, so we didn't have the chance to meet. But I will at the gala. It might be helpful to know a little more about him. He's been with the family for a long time?"

Willow's expression softened. "Oh, yes, dear Yves. We'll lose him soon...he wants to retire, and he has my dad's blessing. Yves had a French mother and a New York dad; both are gone now. For a while, he'd studied Art History at Columbia University, and then he switched to the University of Denver. Before he came here, he'd worked in some small museums and galleries in Manhattan. He also spent some time in Paris, I believe. He never married. Very knowledgeable and private, but well connected. A pleasant man. He made art fun for me, even though I couldn't draw. He has an apartment in Golden but stays a lot in one of our guest houses—the one closest to the pond. Jen-Seng, the gardener, has planted lots of flowering bushes around it. I think it reminds Yves of Monet's gardens."

Diane vaguely remembered the area from her visit for the Monet Exhibit reception. Despite that it was wintertime, the botanical features and fountain had impressed her.

"He goes away sometimes. Short times. He leaves index cards in the door window. Usually, they say TCB or Be Back Soon."

"Where does he go?"

"Oh, somewhere to prospect or make a buy...that's the TCB, Taking Care of Business card. Or, he might go into town, maybe to see a lady friend? Then he posts the Be Back Soon card. We all figured he deserves his privacy and don't pry. He often eats with us, too. He helps throw art receptions. Wears a tux for those during the holidays."

"Indispensable."

"Quite so. When it comes to the family's art collection, he runs a tight ship. He has no trouble telling visitors not to *touch* the paintings." She took a breath. "My dad's deeply indebted to Yves. He's made clever, solid acquisitions. For fifteen years, he's helped my dad put together the collection of his dreams. They've worked on it as a team. My dad would find something he wanted, and Yves would take care of the administrative side for the sale transaction. He even drove to Dallas once to personally pick up a Gauguin painting and brought it home. Or, Yves would spot a good buy and let my dad know. That's what happened with the Monet. The Stonegate Collection is now an investment that's worth many millions, no less, and is covered by Lloyd's of London."

Diane listened with a bit of envy. What a class act. It awed her what deep pockets, like interests, and good intentions could do. Her curiosity still burned.

"Two questions...When will Yves retire? Also, how did Walter meet him?"

Willow stretched her legs out in front of her. Some of the tension Diane had seen in her at first was dissipating. "At the beginning of July. He plans to visit Paris for a while." She pushed her hair away from her cheek. "Would you believe they met at a skeet match at the country club? Yves was a guest of Dirk Greaves, a local art critic. They were all on the same skeet team. Back then, my dad had started his collection with three pieces. He worried about the kind of care they needed, proper display, and building a private collection into what he'd envisioned. Yves had some museum background, and he visited Stonegate the next week at my father's request. A month later, my dad offered him the job. My mom was pleased, too, and the rest was history."

Diane finished writing and smiled. "I look forward to meeting him." Seeing Yves in person would tell her things Willow wouldn't think to notice or share. How he would look someone in the eye, his body language, and his voice would all contribute to Diane's impression of him.

It was equally amazing to Diane how good some folks looked good on paper, or through others' eyes, but turned out otherwise. Still, Aunt Meredith liked him; they'd shared some history and remained friends. That counted for something, too.

Even so, Yves' choice to hang out so closely with Leo and Rydell still puzzled Diane. But that fit for her. She figured this was part of a private investigator's mindset—to walk around being puzzled. The question Why? played a big part in her life.

After Yves retired, these were men who would certainly move to the fringes of his social circle. He *must* be looking ahead to how life would be after his work at Stonegate was over. She surmised he'd move back to Golden. Why, then, would Leo and Rydell, who were still deep into their careers, mean so much to him?

"Do you think he's lonely?" Diane asked.

"Not in your life. Shows no signs," Willow replied. "He reads and keeps himself occupied."

Learning more, Diane concurred with Willow's thinking how their bonding was a stretch. Even the guys knew Yves was leaving. So, what was in this for all of them?

"You'll not miss Yves in the crowd tomorrow night," Willow cut in. "He's tall and has silver white hair now. Likes to wear black jeans and sweaters. He's coming down tomorrow for the gala." She laughed a little. "My mom calls him Mr. Fox. Not to worry, my dad doesn't mind."

Diane threw her a thumbs up. Secure marriages always delighted her.

Willow suddenly glanced at her watch. "Oh, my. I've got to quick get over to Geneva's for Women. Leo's picking me up from there in forty-five minutes." She slid off the stool gracefully. "Geneva has great accessories, and I want new earrings for the gala. One cannot pull off a killer time to remember without the right accessories, right?"

Diane took her point to heart. "Right." Not that it mattered, but Willow and she were from different worlds. To Willow, accessories meant jewelry, sparkly tiaras and belts, or bags, shoes, scarves, or hairclips. But *accessories* had another whole meaning for Diane, P.I. Like, who had the skills needed to pull off a heist, or who was driving the getaway car?

The rap on the storage room door broke up her talk with Willow. She tucked Arabella's journal into her bag and opened the door. "Thanks, again," she called to Willow as she walked away.

Detective McGuire ambled in and slouched against the wall.

"Girl talk?"

"And then some," Diane answered, diverting her gaze. She was carrying concealed hot evidence. By rights, she should be turning it right over to him, except she wanted first shot at it. Badly. But she hedged. A sucker for protocol, she divulged, "Arabella kept a journal. I have it here," she tapped her bag and looked at him meaningfully in earnest. He got the message. "For tonight only?" she added.

McGuire mocked a salute. "Enjoy your late-night reading. Meanwhile, here's something else for you to chew on. The Angelo Barnes and Bob Smith alias search is dead in the water. So, the identity of the guy you'd met in the library about Arabella's daughter is still pending."

"Hmm. Maybe he really is Angelo Barnes. We may never know. But I'm sure he was serious. He'd fully expected to find Arabella there." She followed McGuire down the hall. "On one hand, I wonder how many cosmetic firm families there are in Milan?" referring to the one that had adopted Arabella's daughter. "On the other, we should let sleeping dogs lie."

"What's your gut tell you?" he asked, opening the glass door to the main office. Seemed pretty quiet inside. The parking meter woman was checking out a new batch of tickets, and two teens with blue hair talked with one of the officers.

"That she doesn't factor into this," she said.

"Me, too."

"No use digging skeletons out of the closet," she concluded. "How about finding prints on my love letter?"

An officer from across the room signaled for McGuire. "It was clean. Hold on."

She sighed inside and waited patiently while her fingers itched to open her bag and retrieve what could be the book of answers. Aside from the obvious ones, it'd be really nice to figure out who had tried to do her in up on the trail. She'd filed a complaint with McGuire while she was laid up for observation at Penrose.

The officer handed McGuire a pink message slip. He glanced at it.

"D'you have your cell phone turned off? It's from your husband."

Diane smiled broadly. Anticipation of talking with Tom spiked. "I'm heading home. Meet you in the morning?"

"Tomorrow is Saturday. I sleep in, but since it's you, and it's about this wreck of a case, I'll meet you here. Nine a.m. sharp."

Diane gave him a fist bump. "You're a good man."

McGuire frowned and avoided her gaze. "Not everyone thinks so." He shoved his hands into his pockets. So focused on the case, she hadn't noticed how harried he looked. Something was troubling him.

"My wife wants a divorce," McGuire revealed and shrugged. "But thanks."

"Oh, God," Diane said, halting in her steps. Inside, she wasn't surprised. So many cops' marriages failed. Sadly, it often went with the territory. "Maybe she'll reconsider."

"I'm not so sure...this time. Things change. I'm no longer the man Phyllis needs."

Diane had no words. When a woman had had enough, she was done. Arabella had reached that point with Sam, and Willow was getting closer with Leo. It was a sad revelation that could drift in like a mist or attack like a tiger. Grateful for the man in her life, Diane clutched her phone, knowing she'd soon talk with Tom.

McGuire and she reached the vending machines, and Diane hit one up again for two granola bars and gave McGuire one. "I'm sorry to hear, Detective Roger."

"Classified, for now, Ms. Phipps," he said quietly and stuck the snack into his shirt pocket.

It wasn't the kind of thing she'd pass around anyway, but he waited for confirmation, and she obliged. "Got it."

"Life just sucks sometimes," he added. "Makes us so unsure. See you in the morning." He turned and headed to the front door. It was tough to see a dedicated man in blue who put his energy into getting to the bottom of things to solve cases, struggle for answers about matters of the heart.

She called after him, "One thing *for sure* is that it'll be worth your time."

McGuire turned back toward her and raised his chin. "Why's that?"

She tapped her bag again. "Because I'll know more than I do now. Sleep tight."

He smiled ruefully. "By the way, Undercover Bill says to pull the shades tonight, and...it's not a good idea for you to eat a donut just before you go to bed."

Walking toward him, she squelched her retort. A girl needed at least one occasional guilty pleasure. Yet, she needed to pick her battles. Off-handedly, she asked, "Where's Pete Woodward lately?" as they passed the door to the main office.

"He's on a mission in Denver. He'll be back early tomorrow."

Sensing so, she asked, "Having to do with our case?"

"Everything having to do with the case," he replied shortly. "He's paying a visit to inmate Rouard Clementi."

Diane slowed to a halt. "The infamous forger?"

McGuire nodded deeply. "We need to find out who bought the fake Monet from him and pawned it off onto Walter Haverstone."

She took in a quick breath. She had someone in mind, but kept it to herself. "D'you think he'll sing?"

McGuire answered, "Depends on his mood, I guess. He's not required to. He doesn't have anything to lose at this point, and Pete might get lucky."

She thought for a long moment.

McGuire nudged her arm with his elbow. "You with me?"

Diane raised her hand. "Present. Still, Clementi's customer and the person who made the switch might not be the same guy."

McGuire raised a forefinger. "You don't miss much."

"Thank you, but—"

"And...we have to start somewhere."

McGuire pulled on his cap. Wasn't but a minute passed until he turned away from the front counter and strode toward the front door out of the building, with Diane following closely behind.

"Somewhere like first getting Clementi's confirmation he even painted that particular forgery?" she asked.

"Exactly, despite what our expert Morgan Newberry concluded. Pete took a photo with him." He held the door for her.

"I'm sure Morgan's correct," she said, thinking ahead. "Still, Pete's visit with him isn't so much about admission of forgery, is it?"

"Nope. It's more about the players involved. Somebody's been dealing dirty, killed a woman, and finding out *who* is still at the top of my priority list."

Twenty-one

Time with Tom

Likewise, for Diane. The same goal had driven her days and nights. She was holding more pieces of the puzzle in her hand than ever. Eventually, she could collect them all and lock them into place. However, she wasn't sure she had them all.

The picture coming together so far was ugly, full of deceit, betrayal. In general, motives came in all shapes and sizes. Considering what was up for grabs—a Monet masterpiece—surely greed smoldered at the core of this case.

With all she'd done and learned so far, solving it was nearer at hand for her. Finding out exactly whodunit and how pulled her forward and got stronger with every sunrise. Still, she wasn't counting her chickens. But she would revel in the victory as, at times, her work seemed like she was pitching a war against a powerful dark demon. Coming out the winner always brought her satisfaction, even bragging rights.

Except naming names and motives launched woe and shock for some to bear. Even criminals had unsuspecting friends, family, and employers. So, decent people who cared for perps would suffer. Diane's business was to find answers, but she never had answers for those folks. At best, she could offer a basic hug and condolences.

Tonight, Tom's deep voice soothed her and fired her up at the same time.

"Hello, dear. How's it going?"

Diane nearly melted. She was lounging in an old stuffed chair in the room she designated for her case reviewing. "I'm recovering and am catching up on my reading."

"Recovering? Recovering from what?" Tom asked, audibly tensing.

Not to alarm him, she lightened her tone as she relayed how she'd taken a spill off the trail.

"You fell off a trail?" he repeated, incredulity in his voice. She could just see him shaking his head. "You were hiking alone?" he pressed.

"Well, I thought I was, but not really." She shifted a little, taking some pressure off her sore hip. "I had an assist over the edge."

Dead quiet, then Tom yelled, "What the hell?"

She moved the phone back to her ear. "I'm all right. Really. Just a bit sore and have some bruises. No concussion. Problem is, I'm going to the gala tomorrow evening and need to be looking good and ready for what comes down the pike...like possibly meeting who killed Arabella Laurens mingling in the crowd."

"Yes. You take care of that," Tom encouraged. "When I'm done here in five days, I'll be coming to town to take care of who pushed my wife off a damned mountain." Resolve riddled his tone. "Meanwhile, what're you reading?"

Diane gazed down at her lap. "The victim kept a journal, Tom." She tried to keep her excitement minimal. "I have it for one night. Am meeting with McGuire in the morning. Hopefully, with some new intel. I'm already doubting some folks' integrity. One Monet is worth millions."

Tom chuckled and slipped in, "Hmm. Brings to mind, 'Lead me not into temptation. I can find the way myself,' by Jane Seabrook, an author Aunt Meredith likes."

"Cute," Diane said and grinned. "But, in this case, I believe someone had help finding it."

"Interesting," Tom said after a pause. "Names?"

Diane glanced at the board cluttered with her notes, connector lines, and names.

"Can't say yet, but the list is narrowing." Her voice almost quivered. Premonitions about tomorrow night were kicking in. It happened when she was mere breaths away from turning a case around. Tom caught the subtle quiver. He didn't miss much either.

"You be careful tomorrow night."

"I'll be okay. McGuire's got me covered," she said and tugged on the corner of her shirttail. "Wish you were here, though."

"Five days, dear. Five more days. I miss you, too."

Diane blew him a kiss through the phone. "Did you get that?" she asked playfully.

"Without question," he said quickly. "Look, I've got to run. Sleep good tonight. And do me a favor?"

Time with Tom was fading; she held on to his voice as long as she could. "Of course. What is it?"

He was outdoors from wherever he was calling. The wind was distorting his words. But what came through at the end was, "Take Pearl with you. Promise?"

She assured him she would, and hoped he'd heard her. Naturally, she'd brought along her pistol, safely tucked in her knitting bag. Needing tea, she made some and curled up on the couch with a throw tossed over her legs, as it still got chilly in the evenings.

Twenty-two

The Journal

Diane picked up Arabella's journal and opened the colorful cover. As Willow had reported, the pages were filled with turquoise-inked words. Not surprising, Diane felt, considering her work with art. Her handwriting was consistent from page to page, with the dates noted in the upper right hand corner. Her entries weren't long-winded or wandering. The tone was pleasant and without cuss words. She seemed calm at writing time, non-complaintive, and smooth penmanship formed her words. Diane also noted that Arabella didn't write every day and no pages were torn out. The earliest entry was from the previous summer.

> *July 17. I've been in my studio for three years today! I persist in requesting a little more space for storage from Eugene Ketchum, owner. I've heard there are some cages in a room behind the bakery*

downstairs. Oh, the bakery is divine. They shoot my pastry order up to me via the dumbwaiter. Isn't that cool?

Diane flipped through page after page, ever watchful for names. They appeared often as customers and artists. She'd mentioned places she'd eaten and sometimes with whom, like Pam.

August 5. Pam makes amazing jewelry. I envy her because she starts with nothing and creates mini-masterpieces that last for a long time. I, on the other hand, attend to others' artistic accomplishments. There's no originality from me involved. But I am a caretaker and do save and preserve. And there's a place for that, too.

A smiley face followed.

Diane leafed through more pages with mentions of going to the Front Range Art Society meetings that didn't seem very regular. Labor Day got notes due to a parade she'd been to, and another entry about the weather...early snow, which she didn't mind.

Some shopping notes took space, and when Diane reached the point where she saw Sam Crawford's name, she slowed down. Her description of him would sweep any girl off her feet.

September 20. Sam gives Chris Hemsworth with dark hair a run for his money. His solid hugs make me melt. I met him at Seven Minute Spring Park collecting mineral water. The cap on my plastic jug wouldn't come off, and he helped me. We hit it off. I've been so deep into my work I've had no time— or made no time—to have a special guy in my life. Well, Sam has undone that.

Diane frowned over the little heart she'd sketched by his name. Too bad the outcome had turned toxic.

> *October 12. Sam stood me up for dinner tonight... at least, I think so. I waited for him at the Cliff House for an hour and ten minutes. No call. How long is a girl supposed to wait?*

> *October 15. I'm crushed. My cheek hurts...I told Sam he was being unreasonable about me spending my own money. HE HIT ME! We're done...so done. I called my brother Leo but couldn't reach him...again. That's happening a lot lately. Thank heavens I have my work. It never fails me. Neither does my friend Pam. She's the sister I've never had.*

Diane winced. Gazing through the window into Arabella's life began to sadden her, yet she kept turning pages. "This is my job," she reminded herself aloud. Dark had fallen, and she took a break long enough to set the journal aside and get up out of the comfy chair. Dutifully, she walked around and lowered the blinds to keep Undercover Bill happy. Resettling, she opened the journal again. She found a long expanse of days between dates this time.

> *November 14. Tonight, I'm going to the Front Range Art Society meeting. It's here in town this time, and the program is on Georgia O'Keeffe. Am so looking forward. Last year I had the chance to repair one of her paintings for an owner in Santa Fe. Who gets to do that? ME!*

> *November 14, late. Home from the meeting. A guy walked me to my car with an umbrella because it's*

raining. I'd met him inside during refreshments, and he looked interesting to me. We talked about art, of course. He likes metal art. I guess it was his attire that drew me to him first. Wearing all dark clothing, jeans and a black shirt with silver piping, definitely a country ranch boy. He wore a dark hat, too, and boots and spurs. Dark hair with stubble on his jaw. He smiled great, I will say. Never mentioned his name. There are always regulars at the meetings, but a lot of people meet in passing, too. He was one of those. Just as well. He wrapped his arm around my waist and pulled me in closer under the umbrella. It was starting to hail, and I didn't want to get beaned. Mistake! When we got to my car, he suddenly pressed me up against the driver's door. Then, the dude kissed me. Really hard. I almost threw up. He was a chewer. Said he needed a woman like me. I yelled and wriggled free and pushed hard as I could to back him off. Nobody to help. Surely, God was with me. The creep took off. I've never felt so violated! Never want to see him again. Worries me a little to go to the next FRAS meeting.

Diane remembered her conversation with Jake, the retired jerky shop owner. His sharing helped bring this to the forefront. She took a photo of the written page with her cell phone and emailed it to her computer. Her mind burned with curiosity over who the guy was.

More unnoted days went by in Arabella's journal. Soon, though, entries about James Boyd showed up. They glowed, but were practical, too. As Pam had said, they'd met at the wooden carved bears outside of the Twin Bears shop on Manitou Avenue. Had Arabella met her match? The woman had had enough disappointment that Diane found herself pulling for her.

November 21. James Boyd is my new friend. He has a head on his shoulders and knows art inside and out. His gallery is down the street, and I don't know why our paths haven't crossed sooner. I like him because he understands what I do and my passion for it. He makes me laugh. My work is serious, and it's good for me to laugh. He wears artful sweaters and cord pants. Kind of Ivy League for around here, but works for me. James has a calm manner and knows framing and displays art in his gallery so its best side shows. I like how I feel about me when I'm around him. We're going to the holiday dance together. He seems a keeper, but I've been wrong before. My brother Leo hasn't taken to him, though. I'm not sure why or why he cares so much. Most of the time Leo is tied up with his own business, Willow, and those two men he talks about at Stonegate. One is the curator of the private collection, Yves St. Vrain, whom I haven't met yet, and the other guy I don't know. Oh, Willow is Walter Stonehaven's daughter, and Leo dates her. I thought my only lasting connection to the Stonehavens would be through my work. I'm being considered for cleaning the Monet they have in their collection. Which makes my heart dance! But with Leo so seriously dating Willow, it may happen I'll become even closer to Walter and Ruth Stonehaven. As far as I know, they're all well thought of. Meanwhile, James and I are getting closer with every time we see each other. Like it or not, Leo's just going to have to get used to the idea that I might marry James. I'm in no rush, and time will tell.

Diane smiled.

Twenty-three

An Investigator's Work is Never Done

Burning the midnight oil, Diane was reading more of Arabella's journal when her phone rang. "Yes, Roger McGuire?" she answered with a tinge of dread.

"You're still up," he gruffed. "Lights are on."

She almost rolled her eyes, but she figured he was calling for a good reason.

"Yes."

"I'm calling about the hair the forensics team found at the crime scene."

Well, *that* had merit. "Whose is it?" she asked. After all, this was still a loose end. Another possible puzzle piece of relevance?

"Nobody's. It's a horse hair. Just wanted you to know."

"A horse hair?"

"Yep. Good night." Click.

Diane shook her head. Undoubtedly, the tip fit somewhere. But for now, journal reading took another half hour. Arabella wrote about how Thanksgiving and Christmas had come and gone with little drama. She'd spent holiday time with her parents in Boulder. New Year's Eve with James, and they sealed their relationship with more than a kiss. She was falling for him.

She'd received confirmation that she'd be working on the Monet in early January. The delivery was arranged by Yves St. Vrain through a reputable courier service and approved by Walter Haverstone. Her side note indicated that, as a safety precaution and due to the size and weight of the painting, two drivers would bring it to her on January 7th.

By now, Diane knew differently. Three men were in that van. One of them had a covert job to do, failed, and panicked. She just needed to nail down his identity—beyond doubt.

Diane then read Arabella's last entry twice. Again, Leo had dropped trouble into her lap.

January 4. Leo came by to see me today at work. He's still trying to dissuade me from dating James. There's some kind of trust issue at work here. I told him flat out I would date and marry whom I wanted to. He didn't want to hear it and yelled at me, and I yelled back. I'm sure people could hear us. When the time comes, I want my family's blessing so much. But Leo is not on board. His rejection of James doesn't make sense to me at all. It's like he's hiding something.

January 6. Tomorrow will be the best day of my whole working life!!! I'll be meeting a Monet! I'm so thrilled the Haverstones picked me to do the job. It's a milestone in my career, for sure. Hopefully, a door opener to restore more famous works. Perhaps I'll become the restorer of choice for the MMA in New York! Or one for the Louvre? Yes, unlikely and lofty, but I can dream...

Diane closed her eyes and the journal at the same time. Arabella Laurens had deserved better than catching Leo's disdain and having her life snuffed out. Diane spent the next two hours in her crime case room taking the clue board apart, erasing and re-writing, and rearranging it again and again. She studied the photocopies of the color photos of the crime scene. She also revisited the pictures of Arabella draped over the Monet and how she'd squeezed a tube of paint during her last breathing moments of life.

Many pigment tubes lay scattered near the masterpiece from which to choose. Had she really *chosen* one, or was it by mere chance she'd picked the one she did? Especially since Monet had stopped using such dark hues before his waterlily period?

Baffling, indeed. Until...why Arabella had squeezed a tube of paint at all became crystal clear to Diane. A grand scheme of insidious intent took root in her tired, inquiring mind.

Finally, around 2:00 a.m., she picked up a red marker and drew circles around three names, all solid suspects. Her conclusions weren't pretty. Crime never was. But it could be surprising. She expected some raised eyebrows...and McGuire telling her she needed to go the Front Range Art Society Gala wired. Gladly.

Next, Diane went to the closet and shook out her little black dress. It seemed like an old friend, and time had passed since she'd had an occasion to wear it. She wished Tom would be with her, as it promised to be a fine affair to kick off an exemplary art fair...and her rendezvous with justice.

"Time to celebrate," she whispered.

~ * ~

Diane rose early the next morning to a thunderstorm. The noise rumbled through the mountains while water rushed down the street out front. Sort of unusual, since she'd heard rain usually came in the afternoons or early evenings. But she found the downpour pleasant and reminiscent of home, as rain in northeast Florida was often heavy.

Anticipation for her meeting with McGuire sped up her coffeemaking, shower, and dressing. Her theory about Arabella Lauren's homicide case was double-barreled. She'd gone through all of her jotted notes in preparation. The case had to be airtight before going to court in El Paso County.

There were still a few points, though, about which she was curious and could be important. Arabella had made no mention in her journal about the murder weapon—the beautiful butterfly scarf. Perhaps because she'd received it before she'd started writing about her days?

It could be tied to her killer, or not, hard to say. Next, Diane was still curious about the brownish stain on the scarf. It was hard to believe Arabella would've worn a soiled scarf. There was no blood found at the scene or listed on the medical examiner's report.

She put this on her list to ask McGuire about a forensics update on the murder weapon. The stain might've been left unnoticed by the murderer. Wouldn't be the first time a suspect had tripped himself up this way, leaving behind a personal stamp that sealed a case. The prospect put more spring in her step as she left the little framed house with Arabella's journal in hand.

By the time she'd driven to Detective McGuire's office, the rain had let up. Walking into the building, she smelled coffee and was ready for another cup. To her surprise, Pete Woodrow was sitting next to Roger McGuire at a small worktable. They looked up simultaneously as she entered the room and a round of solemn "Good mornings" followed.

"Pete's back early," McGuire said and gestured for her to take a seat with them.

As she settled, Pete filled her in. "Clementi was somewhat cooperative. He confirmed he'd painted the copy of the Monet, but he clammed up about who it went to. He got all choked up when I showed him the photo of the painting. Says he misses his work." He paused, then, "Roger told me about the journal."

Both men fixed their gazes on her. She'd done her homework and laid Arabella's journal on the table. "Gentlemen, I have some ideas, but not to muddy the waters, I want to withhold them until after the gala this evening. I also have a request to make."

"And it is?" McGuire asked.

"I need an accessory to go with my black dress, and I want to borrow the murder weapon for the occasion."

Unfazed, McGuire handed her a coffee. "You know who murdered her, don't you?" he probed. "Did she reveal the name of someone who scared her or had it out for her enough to do her in?" He picked up the journal and waved it at her.

"Hold on. Arabella had mostly sibling trouble with her brother, and also a few men who'd given her problems, and she'd found a promising mate in James Boyd. She talked of her work and the weather, holiday family times, and nothing about having a daughter, or the scarf, for that matter."

Pete leaned forward. "You want to wear the murder weapon found on the victim's body?"

She nodded resolutely.

"Ma'am, that's downright irreverent." Pete slapped the table top, a growing habit.

"Not meant to offend," Diane said. "But, yes...even though the scarf is stained. Which brings me to ask what kind of stain is it?"

"Coffee?" Pete threw out.

"I doubt it," she replied and held her peace.

McGuire gave her a look. "I'll check with Forensics. I didn't notice it on their report."

"It wasn't. May I borrow the scarf, please?"

McGuire sighed and raised his hand. "I'll go fetch it. Evidence man Eddie is home today."

"You're going to loan it to her?" Pete asked and threw up his hands in disbelief.

Diane raised her chin and met McGuire's met steady gaze.

"She's onto something here," McGuire said. "More than what we've got. So, let her be."

Diane smiled inwardly. Things were going her way. In less than three minutes, McGuire returned with the scarf in its evidence bag. "Don't clean this, or you'll be slapped with tampering." He handed it to her and added, "For the record, I see where you're going with this."

"Yes, to the gala...and straight into—"

"Danger," Pete blurted.

She shrugged. "Simple shock value." She dearly hoped to trip a certain person's switch. At times, shock value was her ally.

"Not alone, she's not," McGuire declared. "Undercover Bill will be at the gala and close by." He nodded at her. "And you'll wear a wire, too."

Diane said, "Thank you. I need to run. I'm getting my hair done." She rose from the chair. "And, by the way, in her own way, Arabella told us who was strangling her."

McGuire and Pete exchanged hopeful glances with each other.

"Can you prove who did it?" McGuire asked point blank, squinting at her.

"I'll be working on it. Trust me."

Twenty-four

Party, Party

Diane checked herself out in the mirror and made an adjustment to the scarf to fold the stain out of view. She was to meet James Boyd at the gallery for the drive into Colorado Springs and checking into the Summit Ballroom at the Hotel Eleganté before 7:00. Picking up her evening bag and depositing Pearl and her ID inside took barely a minute. The wire rested inside the fat knot she'd tied in the scarf.

The weather had improved throughout the day, and she just needed a light wrap for the evening ahead. Truth be told, she had butterflies. This week she'd seen Western art depicting cattle and horse round-ups, but she was about to embark on a round-up of a different kind.

James greeted her warmly at the gallery front door. "You're about to meet some of the best people there are in the art world. Some knew Arabella and her work well. We might catch questions about what happened. She'll be missed at an event like this."

She thanked James again for inviting her further into Arabella's world. "I wish it were for better reasons." She'd covered a lot of investigative ground since James had first invited her to the Gala, but there were still people to meet, like Yves St. Vrain, the curator of the Stonegate Collection. Willow would see to it that they were introduced. Moreover, there was Stonegate's farrier, Rydell, whom Leo had befriended along with Yves.

She agreed with Arabella and Willow that they were a curious trio. Tonight, she'd have a front row seat to watch them interact. Try to accurately decode their bond, understand what made it tick. Usually, things were not as they seemed. It was endemic in cover-ups. Besides what her deductive reasoning had revealed, her deepest intuition told her they weren't just showing up for the sake of appreciating art. Another reason lurked beneath the social surface. Some unfinished business? But Diane could *suspect* all she wanted in her little black dress. *I just need to stay sharp and expose it for what it was: Murder and a grand heist.*

So, when she and James got off the elevator on the fourth floor of the Hotel Eleganté and strolled into the Summit Ballroom, she let her gaze travel the busy room. Across from her the expanse of windows provided a clear view of the Front Range from Cheyenne Mountain to Pikes Peak and beyond. Magical at dusk. Various art displays and tables dotted the room. A dais had been set up near the fireplace where jazz musicians sat in for sets. A small portable dance floor stretched below. Another area was set up with padded chairs theater-style and a podium faced them. Clusters of balloons and streamers wafted overhead.

A waiter dressed in a white shirt, red tie, and dark suit approached Diane and James, offering them wine. James collected two glasses for them as the drink waiter gave Diane a lingering look. His nametag said *Robert,* but Diane nodded at him, sure he was Undercover Bill.

"Thank you," she said calmly.

"At your service, ma'am," the waiter said. "If you should need another, or have a spill, simply wave, and I will return to handle your request." Tonight, he was hatless and his dark hair covered his ears.

Robert obviously kept himself in shape. She spotted the slight bulge under his jacket; he was armed. She had to admit that having a back-up at close range was handy.

James gave her a quick verbal orientation to the artists' stalls and booths in the spacious room with its red, gold, green and blue carpet.

A display of oil paintings caught Diane's eye. "May we?" she asked, and she and James drifted that way. Wending their way through the growing crowd, Diane felt a tug on her sleeve. She found Willow on the other end of the tug. "Hi, so glad you made it," the girl said, her hand tucked under Leo's crooked arm. He greeted her, as well. Willow's emerald green dress and Leo's well-cut grey suit fit in perfectly. Together, they made a stunning couple. James extended a handshake to Leo. "Good to see you again, buddy," he said. Perhaps it was the formality of the occasion, but Diane detected coolness from Leo when he said, "Likewise," and left it at that.

Willow lifted the awkward beat that followed with, "Hey, there's Yves. Let's go meet him." Leo's eyes brightened, and looked in the direction where Willow was pointing.

"Sure, I'd like the chance again," James said. "He's a legend in art circles. The Society just did an article on him in the newsletter about his success and upcoming retirement."

Diane more than welcomed the opportunity. "Yes, let's," she said as the small group moved in Yves' direction. Her steps were sure as James led the way.

Standing near a nature photography display, the Stonegate curator was tall and slender built, looking good in dress jeans. He'd tied his silver-white longish hair into a tail at the nape of his neck. The turquoise shirt and silver bolo he wore set off his well-planed, tanned face. His deep-set chestnut eyes showed years of mixing shrewd business and pleasure.

Yves flashed a smile as Diane and the others drew closer. Willow gave him a brief hug and introduced Diane and James. Realizing what Diane was doing for the family, he adopted a serious tone. "None of us can thank you enough for your service, Ms. Phipps. Such a travesty over one of our Stonegate paintings. No one expected this. Walter and Ruth couldn't be here tonight, but I can assure you not a day goes by without regrets over her loss of life." His face turned sullen, and he shook James' hand. "Again, my condolences."

James's jaw tightened. "I pray for justice."

A silent beat followed.

Yves turned to Diane. "I must say that's a nice scarf you're wearing. Goes well with black." His tone was genuine and his voice revealed no irregularity.

"I thought it a good choice, too," Diane slipped in matter-of-factly, but her pulse rose a tad.

Leo took a second look. "Hmmm. My sister had one like it." Interest shone in his eyes, nothing else. "She was never afraid of color."

"She also had good taste," Willow commented.

That drew a reverent nod from everyone.

"Say," Leo began, "How about we go over to Rydell's display?" Leo asked. "He's done some new work and is getting some People's Favorite votes."

Yves clapped his hands together. "Good idea," and turned that direction for everyone to go along. Being the tallest, he was easy to follow through the crowd. Rydell's space was apparently at the far corner of the room. Yves took it slowly, and Diane walked alongside James. They slowed several times to appreciate other artists' work. Pottery struck Diane as particularly impressive, and James briefly chatted with a copper artist, whereas Willow admired jewelry, and Leo liked the wood carvings.

The drink waiter passed by her again and relieved her of her empty wine glass.

"Would the lady like another?" he asked with decided charm. She could tell he was enjoying his role in those fancy digs. How undercovers changed their personas to fit the scene was commendable. Some deserved Oscars, hands-down.

She declined the wine offer this time and nodded slightly toward the end of the room where everyone was headed. He discreetly tipped an empty wine glass toward her and made a smooth half turn to offer drinks to another cluster of guests.

Meanwhile, James explained more about this special event. "This is an annual *fête* and artists are showing their work by invitation only. So, it's the *crème de la crème* here tonight."

"Is there an auction?" Diane asked, still grateful for the chance to be there.

"Not an auction, per se," James said. "However, there are three more days to follow for the Art Fair. Interested buyers can do business directly with the artists. The exposure for the artists is optimal and business gets brisk. If a buyer expresses keen interest in an item tonight, it is tagged and an appointment is set with the artist for tomorrow afternoon, or later, to complete the transaction. Cash registers are set up for an advertised, open-to-the-public fair."

"Tonight's event is more for artist recognition and having fun," Leo put in, standing on the other side of her. "Are you?" he asked her directly. "Are you having fun?"

Diane dodged his penetrating gaze and put on her best smile. "Of course. This is delightful." They moved on past the pottery and made a slight turn toward the left.

"Ahh, there's Rydell," Yves exclaimed.

Just ahead, Diane glimpsed an array of metal art. As they drew closer, she was able to see the rough boards where metal stars, barbed wire eagles, forged dippers, and gold horseshoes were mounted as if in a barn. The artist had his back to them and was finishing up talking to a man holding a clipboard and handing out ribbons.

Rydell let out a big "Whoot!" as the man gave him a blue ribbon, which he hung on a bison sculpture made partly of black steel wool and wire. The small gathering around him applauded and began to disperse as Diane, James, and all approached.

From behind, Rydell cut a stunning figure. Diane judged him to be about six feet tall with some height added, due to his black hat. His frame was lean and lanky, save for his broad shoulders that hinted of good muscle build beneath his charcoal gray western shirt. His black Levi jeans worked well for him, covering long legs and boot tops.

His hat band and belt matched, proving he paid attention to detail. Rydell exuded a rough-around-the-edges charm and seemed right at home with his wares around him and talking with folks.

Turning around, he smiled broadly first at Yves and then the rest. He had a strong face, and dark hair escaped from under his hat. He pushed the brim back a bit as Willow stepped forward and gave Rydell a hug. Pulling away, she gestured at Diane. "Meet Diane Phipps. She's working on solving Arabella's case."

Rydell stretched out his hand for a shake. A firm shake, at first. "My pleasure. Thank you...We need..." His gaze fell from her face to the scarf as she pulled her hand away. Not even a blink. Rydell cleared his throat. "Yes, we need to...to put the matter to rest. Her death has caused sorrow for us all."

"Yes, it's very disturbing," she began. "I take it you knew Arabella?"

"Not very well, really. We'd met at a function like this."

Diane tilted her head to one side, taking in his sobering expression and dark blue eyes that flickered with concern. Arabella's entry into her journal about the experience rose in her mind. For sure, she was shaking hands with a creep.

"We're doing our best to find our man."

"Man?" he asked, reaching for the bag of Red Man chew lying near his elbow.

"Yes," she confirmed. "It appears so. Prime suspect."

By then, a small bump filled the hollow of his bottom lip. "Good luck, ma'am," he said and tapped the brim of his hat.

Diane stepped back with the others who were fully engaged in admiring his collection of work. She was way into paintings more than she could ever enjoy metal art. But the expression *When in Rome* charged through her mind.

A large wreath made from painted horseshoes caught her eye. There was absolutely no place she could hang it back home. But Aunt Meredith might like to put it on her garage. Except she probably wouldn't want anything from a criminal.

Turned wooden bowls, carved bears and pottery appealed to Diane. Still, she walked over to the wreath for a closer look, which drew Rydell's attention. He ambled over to her. "There are twenty horseshoes in this wreath," he said. "I made each of them. It's my most recent work."

Diane summoned her admiration to report to duty. "How impressive," she said. "I don't know much about a farrier's work or blacksmithing, but this must've taken a while to create."

"About a month," he said, drawing his hand down his stubbled jaw. "In my spare time, when I'm not doing chores."

"Hmm. I see. D'you have a studio?"

He chuckled. "Of sorts. It's in the old tack room in the barn. Walter doesn't mind."

She touched one of the horseshoes. "How'd you learn how to work with horses and the blacksmithing trade. From your father, maybe an uncle, your grandad?"

Rydell glanced down at the scarf and then ceilingward at one of the contemporary overhead lights. His tone turned grave. "No, ma'am. I didn't know my father, my grandad, or if I even had an uncle."

Diane didn't expect his answer and took in a breath. "So, you're self-taught?"

The farrier looked carefully at her. "Not because I wanted to be," he said, lowering his voice. "I was abandoned by my parents. When I was six months old, they put me in a cardboard box, left me in a field one starry Wyoming night and left for parts unknown."

Stunned, Diane shook her head. There were no words.

Rydell went on, "If it weren't for a coyote dragging the box half across the field toward the Coburns' house, and Mrs. Coburn thinking she was hearing a baby cry around midnight, I wouldn't be standing here—let alone shoeing fancy horses, or dreaming about a recording studio."

Rydell's story jarred Diane's senses. Yet she gathered her professional wits. Her mission here was to solve a case. She just still needed undeniable proof. "Well, you certainly have had a rough time of it early in your life. Not much fun to think about."

Rydell walked over and spit chew juice into a plastic cup. "True. Nope, not much. I try not to think about it."

Diane eyed the cup. "Gets you upset?"

The farrier frowned. "Disappointed, even angry sometimes. I mean, who throws away their kid?" He kind of laughed over the absurdity.

Diane sighed. "Just awful." She tapped his arm with her fingertips in sympathy. "Now, I really am interested in this wreath. What's the price, please?"

He obliged her with it and smiled.

"Fine," she said. "Could you put it on hold for me for tomorrow afternoon when the Market opens?"

Rydell couldn't have been more agreeable. "Certainly. I'll put a tag on it right now."

"Perfect," she said.

With that, he turned to the small table behind him, opened a drawer, and pulled out a big red SOLD tag and hung it on the wreath. However, the back of the tag flipped around toward the front as Diane beamed. Her gaze fell to the tag, which read, *Thank you for your business! Blackie Rydell, Metal Artist.*

Diane blinked. "*Blackie?*"

"Yes, it's my nickname."

I'm almost home free! tumbled through Diane's mind.

"Looking forward to tomorrow," she told him.

"Thanks for listening," he said under his breath.

"Sure, anytime. It's good to get things out, and you can tell me more tomorrow afternoon, if you like. I'll not be in a hurry."

She smiled, as if happy with their deal just as James and Willow came up to them.

"Look at my new wreath," Diane chirped and pointed.

Willow replied, "It's amazing. And look at my new earrings."

Pretty they were, and Rydell gave her a fist bump.

"Let's raise a glass," Yves said jubilantly and signaled the drink waiter.

Diane again kept her cool as *Robert* returned to the group with his tray full of libations.

Rydell had another spit into the almost full cup, and Diane nodded to Undercover Bill for pick-up saying, "How about a new spittoon for the gentleman?" Quickly, the dutiful waiter retrieved the cup, saying, "Another, sir?"

Rydell gave a slight bow and accepted a new one, as Diane issued a subtle nod to Undercover Bill. Careful not to spill any tobacco juice on his white gloves, he placed it in a pint-sized, clear plastic bag he'd drawn from his pocket and set the wrapped cup near the rim of the tray. She'd seen hundreds of them...lovely little unmarked evidence bags.

From there, she walked with James toward the weaver's display. "Will you excuse me for a moment?" she asked. "Powder room."

About five minutes later, Diane had the restroom to herself. Lowering her head, she spoke directly into the wire microphone tucked into the scarf knot.

"Have you been getting all of this, Detective McGuire?" she asked. Her cell phone rang.

"Loud and clear," he replied. "Good work."

She turned around and leaned against the sink. "Undercover Bill has the sample. I'm leaving here soon with James. Will drop the scarf off with the PD dispatcher on my way home. A rush request: Need lab confirmation of match by noon tomorrow. We don't want to blow this."

"I'll make a call," McGuire promised. "And Bill needs to drop it off at the lab. He knows where. If Rydell's tobacco spittle matches the stain on the victim's scarf, we'll apprehend all suspects. Before that, I'll need a complete briefing on your conclusions. False arrests aren't an option. Coffee tomorrow morning, nine o'clock, my office."

Diane grinned. "But it'll be Sunday morning."

"Don't be naughty." McGuire clicked off.

Diane touched up her lipstick and rejoined James. A band was playing and people began dancing. For the first time in many weeks, Diane felt like kicking up her heels. If only Tom were there.

Twenty-five

Say again?

Diane reveled in the early morning mountain air. Soon she'd be trading it for sea breeze. Still in her robe, she stepped out onto the small front porch. Her neighbor was baking cinnamon rolls again, which whet Diane's appetite. She was put out of her misery when Marie brought one over to her.

"Fresh out of the oven," Marie said. "How's it going with your case?"

Diane bit into the cinnamon wonder. "I think I'll be leaving here soon."

Marie beamed with understanding. "I don't know how you do what you do. I'd be scared to death to chase down crime suspects. First thing, I'd have to *talk* to them. That alone would be enough to give me the creeps."

Diane nodded with a smile. "There are a lot of snakes out there. But I'm careful, and I'm intuitive and trained. It's also a team effort."

~ * ~

The team meeting in McGuire's office at 9:00 was made up of two people. Diane and him.

"The lab ran the tests overnight," he said. "It's a match."

Relieved, Diane leaned back in her chair. "Then, our work has only begun."

"Want to tell me what you have on this?" McGuire said.

"I might need to call in some help."

Sunday morning at the Manitou Police Department didn't have a lot of traffic. Still, they'd keep their voices low and tones grave. It just seemed to go with the topic. In some ways, Diane felt it was almost clandestine. She pulled out her little notebook where she'd listed what she believed had happened and why. She would bank on her list of suspects. It was the kind of certainty that first came from an unknown place down deep inside her. It never failed. Employing follow-up, rational fact-finding minimized doubt. Her spirit, energy, and intellect shared the same page on whodunit. But coffee was needed first, and McGuire shared that opinion.

"Be right back." He got up and went out the door.

Diane once more checked her notes. Minutes ticked by, then the door reopened slowly. She looked up to find McGuire showing Leo Laurens into the room.

"We have company," McGuire said, carrying three cups of java.

Diane took in a short breath in surprise.

"Leo," she greeted, noting his appearance.

"Hi," he grunted and slumped into an empty chair on the other side of the table.

Diane leaned forward. "Are you okay? Is Willow all right?"

Resting his elbows on the surface and splaying hands out, he looked at her.

"I gotta talk to you." His words slurred.

"Coffee?" she offered, keeping her voice even.

"Wouldn't hurt."

McGuire put a cup in front of him and sat next to Diane. Leo ran a hand through his hair.

"Did you have a rough night?" McGuire asked.

Leo slurped it black. "More like a rough six months. Thanks for this."

Diane crossed her arms and lifted her chin slightly. It'd been a whole night since she'd talked with a criminal. "What's going on?"

"I've been up all night. Tried to find Willow. Had some beers."

Diane nodded. "Tried to find Willow?" she repeated.

"She got pissed at me and left. Yves wanted to take Rydell and me for a drink not too long after you left the gala. Willow wanted to stay and dance. I asked her to wait, and told her I wouldn't be long. But we went over, had three drinks." He pulled out his cell phone and checked for messages. "Yves is about to retire, you know."

"Yes," Diane said. "I do know."

He repocketed the phone. "Willow was gone when I got back to the ballroom. I went to our room, but her stuff was gone. She'd checked out of the hotel." Leo shook his head. "She just doesn't understand."

McGuire shrugged. "You want us to try to find her?"

Diane set her cup aside. Leo was visibly bristling with nerves.

"Is this why you're here?" she asked simply.

The room fell quieter than quiet can get.

"You'd asked me about my night," he said roughly.

"So, why *are* you here?" Diane coaxed; her gaze locked on him.

Leo straightened and cleared his throat as best he could.

"I know who killed my sister."

McGuire gave him a minute and then said, "So do we."

Leo's eyes widened as Diane said, "But we'd love to hear your version. So, go ahead and dish. We might've missed something."

McGuire let him know he was recording from this point on. "No offense, but sometimes my memory isn't as good as it should be," he said.

"Why not start at the beginning?" Diane said, opening her notebook to a new page.

Leo frowned at her. "Look, I already know I'm not leaving here." He dropped his car key and wallet on the table. "But I've lost my sister—even though we didn't get along so good, she was blood—

and *now* my girlfriend has split. Got to me, you know? Money isn't everything. Time to cut bait. Salvage what I can out of this shit."

"Even if it's ten million dollars?" Diane probed. "That'd been your share of the value of the Monet when it sold."

Leo gave her a thumbs up and also pulled out a small, thin black book and set it beside his keys. "Last night you showed up wearing my dead sister's scarf...that took cajones." He snickered. "Hell, it was a shakedown, of sorts. The heat was on. You were on to us. It was only a matter of time 'til we all went down. Right, Ms. Phipps?"

Diane sighed. "Right as rain."

"You know what I need?" Leo asked suddenly. "Another beer."

McGuire laughed. "Fresh out. How does St. Vrain fit into this?"

Leo's eyes darkened. "First, he's Walter's curator and most trusted employee. Yves bought the Monet years ago so he could steal it. He needed a really good forgery to pull off a switch."

"So he contracted Rouarde Clementi to paint one," Diane said and rested her chin on the heel of her hand.

Leo winked. "You've done your homework, haven't you?"

"That's why she's here," McGuire stated. "But go on. How'd *you* get into this?"

"Yves couldn't make the switch alone. With the frame, it's a heavy painting. Rydell and I personally drove the original to a warehouse and made the switch. Then, one day not long after that, Walter up and decided he wanted his Monet cleaned. It got discussed. Yves had somebody in mind for the job. Somebody he knew who owed him a favor. But sweet Willow suggested my sister. Walter agreed. Then, things got dicey."

"Arabella would figure out the painting was a fake," Diane interjected.

"That's where I came in again. My sister really wanted to go back to Italy for a fun trip. But she didn't have the money. So, I put up ten thousand in hush money. Next up was how to get it to her. Walter played right into our hands when he wanted someone he knew and trusted to ride along with the security courier service. So, he hit up Rydell for the job."

"Except Rydell didn't want the job," Diane said.

Leo raised an eyebrow. "How'd you know that?"

Diane quipped, "I read a lot."

McGuire rolled his eyes.

Leo resumed, "Walter can be persuasive when he wants to be. But sending him was a mistake. See, Walter didn't know Rydell had made a bad impression on my sister the night he tried to feel her up in the parking lot after a F.R.A.S. meeting. She wouldn't want to be within fifty feet of him again."

"She refused the money," McGuire said.

Leo nodded. "The farrier has a short fuse, and that tripped his switch. So, he...he..."

"He strangled her with her own scarf," Diane finished for him.

Leo fell quiet. Deep remorse clouded his eyes. "Yes, ma'am."

"The painting was left behind because it had little to no value," McGuire added.

"And too heavy for one guy to carry, even with a dolly," Leo said. "But for the record, the gilded frame was worth five thousand dollars."

McGuire whistled.

"My stupid sister," he almost yelled. "All she had to do was take the money. Who wouldn't want ten thousand bucks a month for five years? I negotiated that amount with Yves for her!" Leo got up, lurched toward the left, and sat back down. "Anyway, Walter was devastated when he found out his Monet was fake and a woman had died cleaning it. I don't think he'll ever recover."

Diane's thoughts jumped ahead. *Walter Stonehaven certainly won't be, knowing he was betrayed by those men he so trusted. Moreover, Aunt Meredith won't believe it, but Tom will help her.*

McGuire cut in. "Why didn't you guys just send the real Monet down here? Do the switch after she cleaned it? Could've avoided all this."

"I suggested that, but Yves said there were about eighty-five reasons not to."

"And they were?" Diane asked.

"That's about how many miles it is from Walter's to Arabella's studio. Eighty-five ripe chances for someone to hijack thirty-four million dollars' worth of art on the way. Yves didn't want to chance it."

"But y'all *chanced* it with Arabella Laurens."

Leo shrugged. "A woman who knows too much can be controlled."

Diane grimaced. Disgust seeped up into her mouth like bitter bile. Leo's only saving grace was that he was confessing. Instead of dumping her civil upbringing and spitting on him, she asked quietly, "And where's the original Monet now?"

Leo tapped the little black book with his forefinger. "Yves found a buyer four days ago. Grand Caymans. But I don't know who the buyer is, or where the Monet is now. My part's done. I'm done with all of this. Get it?"

Done...except for the consequences, Diane thought.

McGuire shook his head. "Not quite. It'll be your words about the theft against St. Vrain's when we pick him up."

Leo looked hard at them both. "Here's your proof." He pushed the small black book toward Diane. It reminded her of the bank passbook her grandmother had for her savings account. "This is why Yves wanted to have drinks last night. He gave Rydell his, and me mine."

Bingo! Diane thought. *The unfinished business!* She opened the book. "There's a string of numbers in here."

"It's my personal code to access the Swiss account in my name. That's where my cut sits."

Leo wore the same black dress pants and blue shirt he had worn last evening. "I wish I knew where Willow is."

"Does she know about any of this?" McGuire asked.

"Nope. This deal was between Yves, Rydell, and me. By the way, you won't find Blackie at the market this afternoon. He split last night."

"Where'd he go?" McGuire demanded.

Leo winced. "What's your rank here?"

"Lieutenant."

"Well, with all due respect, Lieutenant, you're looking at a gift horse in the mouth here. I don't know where the hell he went."

McGuire opened his mouth and shut it again, which Diane figured was pretty smart. Because it looked to her like he was about three beats away from reading this guy his rights and throwing him in the little slammer meant to hold one town drunk, two at the most. But she wasn't quite done with Leo.

Diane raised her hand. "Personally, I want to thank you for cooperating like this. It'll be taken into consideration come trial time. Also, I do have another question."

Leo half-smiled and trained his gaze on her. "Shoot."

"What was your problem with James Boyd?"

Leo opened his hands palms up. "I had no problem with him as a person. But he was too risky; he knows art better than Walter knows aluminum. Bringing James into the family would put him closer to the forged Monet. None of us wanted him to find the flaw and get too curious."

Flaw? Diane unfolded her hands in front of her. "Excuse me? There was a flaw?"

Leo leaned back and crossed his legs. "I said Yves found a good forgery, not a perfect one."

"Say again?" McGuire blurted.

"There's a missing water lily bud. Pink, near the lower left-hand corner. Good chance James' keen eye would've caught it someday, and the whole damn gig would've been up. It was up to me to see that didn't happen. So, I gave Arabella grief about him."

Satisfied, Diane closed her notebook. "Just one more thing. Who pushed me off Eagle Path?"

Leo averted his gaze. "Rydell. He was in town early for the gala. Yves thought you needed a strong hint to leave." He then pushed himself up out of the folding chair. "I'm done." Turning toward Diane, he added, "I heard you went for a good tumble and looked like it. But I gotta say, lady, you clean up good."

Twenty-six

Winding Down

Diane showered and wrapped herself in her robe that night. She was privately celebrating another CASE CLOSED. Tom would be proud of her again. Yet her smile was slow to come. Roger McGuire had called her about an hour earlier.

"Our holding cell is full. Four of them in there," he began. "We've apprehended the whole bunch. Transport to Denver arranged for the morning."

"Where'd you find Blackie?" she inquired.

"In Soda Springs Park, looking scruffy and hanging out with the sometimes homeless. Undercover Bill tagged him. Pete brought in Yves St. Vrain. He was checking out of the hotel and tried to make a run for it, but Pete tackled him in the lobby."

Diane shook her head. "Good work. Wait...who's the fourth in holding?"

"Ha, here's a kicker for you," McGuire said. "Willow Stonehaven."

"What?" she exclaimed. "How'd *that* happen? I figured she took a bus back home."

"She's hooked up with Blackie Coburn now. Found together under a picnic table. She resisted arrest. Coburn told her to knock it off. She didn't, and he smacked her on the butt. Now she's filing an assault complaint against Coburn."

Diane rested her hand on her hip. "I don't know whether to laugh or cuss."

How could things get so messed up? She could half see how a woman thought Rydell "Blackie" Coburn was hot. But his values were not.

It took all kinds of people to make up the world. Buyer beware. Willow's rough ride was only beginning.

For Diane, the case was solved: Grand theft with a senseless murder attached. Motive: Greed. Suspects: Arrested. Evidence and Proof: Secured.

Churned her up inside to think of it. Yet, time had come for her to let go. Enough. She could figure out wrongdoings, make people accountable for them, but she couldn't rid humanity of its demons.

"Well, it's what we got," McGuire summed up. "When're you leaving?"

"Tom and I will go up to Denver at the end of the week. Then, it's back to Atlantic Beach for us."

McGuire paused. "I just want to say thank you. You filled in the gaps where we didn't know there were gaps. You didn't misstep once. Not once. You're a real pro, Diane Phipps. Stop by here before you go?"

She promised she would. It'd give her the opportunity to introduce Tom. Networking with other crime fighters was like extending one's family. The more, the merrier.

~ * ~

Diane opened the front door two days later, and Tom strode in and embraced her. She molded herself to him and soaked up his warm kiss, masculinity, and spirit.

"You okay?" he asked huskily.

Funny how she could stand tall and aloof around crooks, but melted for her husband. When Tom came back home from an assignment, she always gave thanks. Their work worlds threw them into chaos based in treachery, deceit, and even danger. But they had each other when they crawled back out.

"I'm better now," she murmured. "You?"

"I'm best now." He pulled back a bit, still holding her. "I brought you something, and I'm off work for the next month."

Just off the case, Diane smiled and figured the universe might be rewarding her. "I love good news. What'd you bring me?"

Tom released her, headed out to the front porch, and brought in his bag. "I made a side trip to Estes Park on my way back to you." He unzipped the top, pulled out a plastic bag, and tossed it to her. "This is as fresh as it gets."

Diane caught it mid-air and cried with delight. "Salt water taffy!"

~ * ~

By Saturday afternoon, Diane and Tom were sitting with Aunt Meredith at her kitchen table. Aunt Meredith brushed a tear away from her cheek with a tissue. "You know, you go along thinking you know someone, but one day you wake up and find out you don't!"

Tom reached over and patted her arm.

"I don't know how people get so pulled off track," she lamented. "Yves was a good guy, a friend. I liked him."

Diane's heart went out to her. "Of course, you did. He wanted everyone to like him. He worked at it."

"He was an operator, Aunt Merrie," Tom added.

"Maybe now, but he wasn't always." She sniffled. "At least he didn't kill that poor woman." She rose from the chair, cut another piece of apple pie and set it down in front of Tom. "Thing is, now I don't trust my own judgment. He made a fool out of all of us who had faith in him."

Tom helped himself to a forkful. "If it's any consolation, he'll be paying for his own misjudgment for quite a while."

Aunt Meredith sighed. "*His* misjudgment?"

"Sure," Diane said. "He thought he could get away with it."

"That's what criminals have in common," Tom said. "All of them."

"Well, when I called you two for help, I certainly wasn't expecting this kind of outcome," Aunt Meredith said. "But I can see now it was one of the best calls I ever made to anybody."

Tom threw Diane a wink. "True. Good judgment on that one, and my wife deserves the credit for solving the case."

"But she's *your* aunt," Diane countered, sipping coffee. "I wouldn't have come out here otherwise."

"Maybe," Tom teased. Diane scrunched her nose at him. He knew she loved challenges and was a sucker for sinking her sleuthing teeth into a tough case.

"The good news is that the Monet's been traced and found," she shared. "Walter and Ruth are over the moon." She dabbed her mouth with an ecru monogrammed napkin. Aunt Meredith enjoyed fine things. "It's a sewed-up-tight case. Detective McGuire called to say that both Leo's and Rydell's fingerprints were identified on the three one-hundred-dollar bills left behind."

Mostly satisfied, Diane added a dollop of freshly whipped cream onto her pie. Only one curious detail had evaded her wanting to know all the answers. Did Arabella really have a daughter? It certainly appeared to be true. But, in reality, not everything was as it seemed. Time and distance had separated her from learning the hushed truth about Francesca. Still...

Meredith fell quiet and gazed out the window at the mountains in the distance. She lived a rather sheltered life. Being so close to the ugliness of this homicide and theft had to be taking a toll on her gentle spirit.

"You okay, Aunt Merrie?" Tom asked.

She gazed back at him and raised her chin. "Not to worry." Her pink sweater had slipped from her shoulder, and she pushed it back into place. "I just have some memories to erase."

Tom got up and hugged his aunt. "Good. And you have a pie recipe to give to Diane."

"Please?" asked Diane.

Aunt Meredith's pale blue eyes twinkled. "I'm going to miss you two."

Twenty-seven

About Francesca

Diane turned the calendar to another new month, June. She'd been back home for eight weeks since she and Tom had returned from Denver. He'd left again last night on a new covert assignment in Oregon. This time, a cult was systematically poaching wildlife.

Diane had arrived at her office early this Thursday morning. She'd done the follow-up work on the Arabella Lauren case there. Computer reports were finished, and the commendation letter to her from the mayor of Manitou Springs had been filed. Tom's salt water taffy gift had all been eaten, too.

Feeling restless, she yearned for a new case. Until somebody's world erupted again and they wanted help, there was only one thing left for her to do that'd keep her close to home and busy—she'd knit another scarf.

She walked over to the corner of the desk where her knitting basket waited. Nicely enough, Aunt Meredith and she had gone shopping while she and Tom had stayed for three days before coming home. A good yarn shop had offered colorful fine yarns, some spun in Iceland, Australia, and Canada. Diane's taste leaned toward soft hues of gray, lavender, rose, and moss.

She moved Pearl aside from its resting place inside the basket and pulled out a skein of Moss worsted wool. Using her US No. 10 bamboo needles, she cast on 26 stitches. It wouldn't take her long to finish a scarf for Aunt Meredith for Christmas.

An hour or so passed as Diane lounged in her comfortable yellow chintz chair in front of her desk, when a knock roused her from counting stitches. Setting the work aside, she answered the door. A young woman, wearing sunglasses and a fashionable floppy hat, stood on the step.

"Excuse me," she began, "but I'm looking for a Ms. Diane Phipps." She pointed to Diane's shingle hanging out on its weathered post.

Diane confirmed she'd found her. "I'm Diane. May I help you?" The more Diane looked at her, the more familiar she looked. Tallish, dark long hair, slender build. She carried a leather woven bag and wore a sleeveless powder blue dress with flat white buttons all the way down the front. Expensive Italian toeless shoes finished off her polished appearance.

"We've never met," the woman said with a slight accent. "And it doesn't seem quite right for us not to meet."

The heat and humidity of the day was already on the rise. Diane opened the door further.

"Please come in, or we'll both wilt."

She led the guest into her office with its hurricane blind windows and orchid plants.

"Perhaps you want to give me your name?" she said over her shoulder. "I usually see new clients by appointment, but I'm free this morning, and we can chat. Come have a seat." She gestured toward the yellow chintz chair, where prior clients had sat and poured out their stories to her.

Her guest remained standing. "I'm not a client, Ms. Phipps. My name is Francesca Pretoria Alberici. You knew my mother, at least, sort of...Arabella Laurens. Rather, you found the person who took her life."

Diane widened her eyes. "Yes...yes, I did," she said, leaning against the front edge of her desk for support. So it was true. Arabella had been a mother. Looking more closely at the girl, she said, "I see her in you. I'm so, so sorry, she—"

"Mr. Barnes informed me. He is my family's courier and confidant. He accompanied me here to the states. My family owns a cosmetic firm in Milan. I help with package design and new business development. We're here for a cosmetic show in Fort Lauderdale. It was my idea to find you, and he agreed to it."

Diane smiled. "Mr. Barnes? We'd spoken in Manitou Springs. I'd given him the news about your mother. I tried to find him again, but couldn't."

Francesca nodded. "He likes privacy, but he let me know about what had happened," she said, moving toward the chair. "Maybe I will have a seat."

"Sure. Please," Diane offered. She stepped around to the back of the desk and sank into her office chair. There were some mornings that getting up really paid off. This was one of them.

"I want you to know your mother was highly regarded. She had two very good friends who still mourn her loss today." She then told her surprise visitor about James and Pam.

Francesca looked at her soulfully while she talked. Tears welled up in her brown eyes. She pulled a lace-edged hankie from her purse, which she kept at her side on the cushion. "My mother and I had never met. Mr. Barnes was laying the groundwork for that to happen, though. Not here. I mean, in Italy, where I live. She'd studied there, you know."

Diane agreed that she did. "Her brother Leo had mentioned that she wanted to go back." She decided to leave out the context in which it was mentioned, that being he'd said it during his confession about the murder of his sister. This girl seemed a bright and sensitive sort. She already had lost her mother. Even though she'd grown up separated from Arabella, efforts were made to connect through the years through Mr. Barnes.

"My Uncle Leo deserves what he gets for his part," she stated matter-of-factly. "Thank you for making it happen. This is why I'm here. To thank you...in person."

Diane slowly leaned forward and stretched her arm out across the desk as Francesca reached for her hand from the other side. "I know the police were doing all they could, but *you* made the difference, Ms. Phipps."

Diane's heart gave a resounding thump. Releasing Francesca's hand, she said modestly, "Sometimes all it takes is fresh eyes."

Francesca reached into her bag and pulled out a rectangular box wrapped in blue fabric.

"Maybe so, but I'll always be indebted to you for your attention to my mother's case," she said and handed Diane the box. "And I have this for you."

Diane's eyes misted. "It's just what I do."

Francesca regarded her quietly for a moment, and then, "What you'll find in there is unique...actually, it's rare. A treasure. I've had it for quite a while...years. My family purchased it for me at a private auction in Paris. It's authentic. Considering its nature and what you've handled in your work to find my mother's killer, I feel its rightful place is with you and belongs in your care. So, I'm leaving it with you and thanking you."

Grateful beyond words, Diane wrapped her fingers around the longish box. The container was lightweight and the cloth silky. No ribbon adorned it, and the wrap job wasn't the neatest. But the sparkle in Francesca's eyes told Diane it was from the girl's heart. She'd already been handsomely paid by Walter Stonehaven, but how could she not accept Francesca's gift? In a way, it represented closure for Arabella's daughter. She wouldn't deny anyone of that.

"May I open it now?" Diane asked softly.

Francesca scooted closer to the edge of chintz covered chair. Anticipation brightened her face. Brushing strands of wayward hair away from her check, she said, "Please."

Diane got to it and soon laid aside the wrapping. Sitting on the desk in front of her, the long, old box waited. The gold fleur-de-lis stamp on the thin lid was partially worn away. Carefully, she lifted the top, set it aside, and found tissue paper inside holding something dear.

While the palm tree fronds outside the window bobbed in the sea breeze, her curiosity piqued. Tearing away the tissue, Diane found a long, used paintbrush in her hand. The wooden handle thickened as it neared the crimp of the silver ferrule that held the heel of the plump, hair tuft almost reduced to stubble.

She picked it up and twirled it between her fingertips. "A paintbrush?"

Francesca brushed away a tear. "A Monet paintbrush. From his years at Givenchy. My mother loved Monet. Again, I want you to have it."

Diane laid the brush back in its tissue cradle. "I don't know what to say," she said, her voice wavering. "Except that this probably belongs in a museum."

Francesca smiled. "It came from a small museum that had been almost destroyed by fire. Their auction was held to raise funds for rebuilding. My stepfather donated and had paid handsomely for it. Now, it's yours."

"Thank you," Diane said, knowing that wasn't enough.

Francesca gathered her bag and stood. "I must go. Mr. Barnes will be picking me up in another few minutes. After the cosmetic show is over, we'll return to Milan. It's been nice meeting you. He said you were nice."

Diane rose from the chair and stepped around to the front of her desk. After a brief hug, she walked Francesca to the front door. "I'll take good care of the brush," she said. "Good luck with your show."

Francesca stepped off the porch and waved. "If you should ever come to Milan, find me. Until then, *ciao.*"

It was times like this that Diane harbored not one shred of doubt she'd chosen the right path for her own life's work. It was never easy. Fighting crime was full of educated guesswork, instinct, intuition, logic, following clues, suspects, ferreting out secrets, having courage, writing reports, training, sorting out false leads, late night work, grit, knowing law, focus, commitment, surprises, science, and perseverance.

Like colors, they all fit on a palette. In quiet reflection, Diane figured she was no Monet. But a case solved by her was still her own carefully-crafted, original work of art.

Meet Karen Hudgins

Karen Hudgins has always loved stories--in all their form--and settled into writing fiction about 19 years ago. She particularly likes creating characters and settings, making the places seem like characters. Born in Pennsylvania (Lancaster County), her life has offered her chances to live in the South, the Mid-West, and now the West in Colorado.

She first devoted her spirit, creativity, and imagination to learning the craft of writing by creating contemporary, single-title romance full-length novels, exploring the ups and downs of true love with happy endings. Seven of them.

Her latest efforts have shown up in the Mystery Section with the Diane Phipps, P.I. series. She is sticking with happy endings because Diane fights the good fight and solves stubborn cold cases.

Karen has a B.S. in Behavioral Science, which comes in handy for writing about story people. She's a mom, a grandma, and her ginger cat's best buddy. When not writing, Karen likes photography, gardening, music, movies, time with people, Nature, and her book club. She's active on Facebook, keeping connected to friends, former classmates, co-workers, and family. She's currently working on her eleventh mystery novella.

Other Works From The Pen Of

Karen Hudgins

Death of a Mermaid – Murder in Paradise? Diane Phipps, intrepid P.I., uncovers secrets, faces danger at Blue Wave Resort, and solves a perplexing case—the death of Mermaid Nerissa.

Secrets of the Heart – Molly, boutique owner, secretly believes she's fallen from grace and doesn't deserve goodness like compassionate Julian, master coffee roaster, who also has troublesome secrets—but brews up irresistible true love for her.

When Hearts Speak – Sarah Grace, recently, widowed, follows her passion for watercolor painting, which leads her to handsome, enigmatic Wyatt, who slowly reveals his dark torment and love.

Best Man – After a polo accident, a wedding couture designer tangles with her client's Best Man, a vintner and polo player, who ultimately becomes her best man for life.

Tonight with Tarzan – An interior designer falls for a local "Tarzan", whose work and secret dual identity pushes her to overcome fears—or lose the love of her life.

Midnight with Maverick – A pastry chef and copper fortune heir find true love despite their backgrounds and the mystery that rocked their families apart twenty years ago.

One Night with Zorro – A lace proprietor finds the man to fulfill her dreams—except an almost fatal tragedy steers him away from what she also fervently wants—*children*.

Next Year's Promise – Betrayed in love, a promotions professional vows never to mix business and romantic pleasure again, but meets a handsome Australian sheep rancher who tests this pledge.

Letter to Our Readers

Enjoy this book?

You can make a difference

As an independent publisher, Wings ePress, Inc. does not have the financial clout of the large New York Publishers. We can't afford large magazine spreads or subway posters to tell people about our quality books.

But, we do have something much more effective and powerful than ads. We have a large base of loyal readers.

Honest Reviews help bring the attention of new readers to our books.

If you enjoyed this book, we would appreciate it if you would spend a few minutes posting a review on the site where you purchased this book or on the Wings ePress, Inc. webpages at: https://wingsepress.com/

Made in the USA
Columbia, SC
04 May 2021